The
Last Will &
Testament
of Zelda McFigg

The
Last Will &
Testament
of Zelda McFigg

BETSY ROBINSON

Black
Lawrence
Press

Black
Lawrence
Press

www.blacklawrence.com

Executive Editor: Diane Goettel
Book design: Amy Freels
Cover design: Angela Leroux-Lindsey
Cover and interior art: Betsy Robinson

Published 2014 by Black Lawrence Press.
Printed in the United States.

Praise for *The Last Will & Testament of Zelda McFigg*

I couldn't put it down...I was amazed at the originality...I enjoyed how Zelda made it through the world. She is a person I've never, in my wildest imagination, ever known before.

—Jonathan Storm, former critic for *Philadelphia Inquirer*

In the deft, witty, highly conscious hands of novelist (and theatre veteran) Betsy Robinson, the excruciatingly wild ride of *The Last Will & Testament of Zelda McFigg* becomes an act of seduction. (And Zelda thought she was writing a memoir!) Never staying in one place too long, which is more than can be said of its anti-heroine, Zelda, the novel's tone is as reliably unreliable as all of its scarred characters. If there is really nothing to hang on to, it must be a little like life, or death, or trying to create something. Betsy Robinson is alive, and kicking.

—Estha Weiner, poet and professor

I *loved* this novel! The writing is glorious, the vocabulary a delight to follow. I laughed—I rooted, I could not put it down. It's unique and funny and odd and beautiful. Two writers have made me laugh out loud: Martin Amis and David Sedaris. Now Betsy Robinson!

—Maureen Phillips, TV producer

The Last Will & Testament of Zelda McFigg is an entertaining novel about a woman who spends her life trying to find herself. With no role model other than a down-and-out poet, she goes off into the world to seek out survival methods. Along the way, she meets numerous obstacles to success and memorable characters. She is often her own worst enemy, yet she perseveres. Her self-portrait

is real, down to the blemishes, and despite everything, the reader is rooting for her. Betsy Robinson has written a story that rings true when life does not go according to plan and she has given us wonderful three dimensional characters who will be remembered long after the last page is read.
—Devin McKay, M.L.S., M.A., deputy chief librarian, Queensborough Community College

As a veteran of 36 years as a high school library media teacher and a member of a number of book clubs, I found *The Last Will & Testament of Zelda McFigg* to be a rollicking romp. The development of the characters seems true to life in a demented sort of way, and involves more than one ironic twist. In an off-the-wall style reminiscent of Vonnegut and Brautigan, Robinson interjects many "where-did-that-come-from moments" into her book. You scratch your head, and then you smile.
—John Volkman, librarian, Fresno schools

The
Last Will &
Testament
of Zelda McFigg

We are the one part of creation that knows what it's like to live in exile and that ability to turn your face toward home is one of the great human endeavors and great human stories.
—David Whyte

Little book, you will go without me—and I grudge it not—to the city. Alas that your master is not allowed to go! Go, but go unadorned, as becomes the book of an exile; in your misfortune wear the garb that befits these days of mine. You shall have no cover dyed with the juice of purple berries—no fit colour is that for mourning; your title shall not be tinged with vermilion nor your paper with oil of cedar; and you shall wear no white bosses upon your dark edges. Books of good omen should be decked with such things as these; 'tis my fate that you should bear in mind. Let no brittle pumice polish your two edges; I would have you appear with locks all rough and disordered. Be not ashamed of blots; he who sees them will feel that they were caused by my tears.
—Ovid's *Tristia, Book I: The Poet to His Book*
    (Arthur Leslie Wheeler, trans.)

...my meditation would become truly stable only when I concentrated on the black light. I felt peaceful, but at the same time I was so eager to know what I was going to see next that my mind was not as quiet as it might have been. During this period I would see in meditation a deep and terrifying darkness such as I had never seen in the outside world. This darkness made me frightened of meditating, but even so, I would remain in it for long periods at a time.
—Swami Muktananda, *Play of Consciousness*

A human being is a part of the whole, called by us "Universe," a part limited in time and space. He experiences himself, his thoughts and feelings as something separate from the rest—a kind of optical delusion of his consciousness. The striving to free oneself from this delusion is the one issue of true religion. Not to nourish it but to try to overcome it is the way to reach the attainable measure of peace of mind.

With my very best wishes,

sincerely yours,

Albert Einstein

—Letter to Robert S. Marcus (February 12, 1950)

I'm in a place where I don't know where I am!... D'oh!

—Homer Simpson, *The Simpsons*

Prologue

Dearest Reader:

My name is Zelda McFigg, and, until recently, I weighed approximately two hundred thirty-seven pounds. I am four foot eleven inches in stature, and I have not had sex. Ever. Also, I have never been anybody's favorite, and this last fact, in my opinion, is an injustice of the highest order perpetrated by all persons I have ever met.

Before I begin the tale of the unforgivable and thoughtless actions of everyone from my neglectful parents to the lunch delivery lady who, yesterday, mumbled insouciantly at my request for lightly salted snacks and then sneered at her twenty-five cent tip, which, believe me, for a forty-nine and one-quarter-year-old in my circumstances, is generous—before I begin, there are a few things you must know about me:

Although I have found legitimate fault with most humans, I have been a contributing member of society. As a teacher of seventh grade English, to be precise. For nearly three decades I instructed ungrateful provincial juvenile delinquents in the art of self-expression and proper punctuation until I was forced to retire almost two years ago during the depth of the recession. Yes, I was a dedicated educator, a profession deemed one of the most important in the universe by the most popular television hostess in the world—an African American lady with a weight problem similar to my own, whom I will call Miss Olga. But I will get to her later.

I am writing this memoir not only to set the record straight, but to make a confession: due to the dearth of respect as well as the larceny I have experienced at the hands of everyone in a position to showcase my unique talents, I was forced to pursue alternate routes to survival. I lived under what another self-educated artiste, Mr. Jack London, called "the law of club and fang," creatively adjusting to changing conditions in the ruthless struggle that is required of feral animals and humans working in capitalist systems where worth and status are assigned in correlation to pleasing or less-than-pleasing appearances. As a master of invention, I have done things that some of you may judge harshly. Therefore, I have one request: please suspend those judgments until you have considered my entire story.

Chapter 1

My mother, who was a morning person, never understood my waking fear. As far back as I can remember I've had it: At the buzz of the alarm clock, I'd be electrocuted into consciousness, my heart in my mouth, my room inundated by my stink. (A genetically determined bad body odor which erupts much like a skunk's when I feel threatened or humiliated; it is a sour, pungent smell that cuts through deodorants, antiperspirants, and every perfume and toilet water known to womankind. I have learned to accept myself with this condition and negotiate it via quick trips to ladies rooms for sink rinses with a special antibacterial soap that, to this day, I order in purse-size bars from a catalog, which name I will not divulge for reasons that will eventually become apparent.) Heavy with dread, I'd make my way to our wretched mouse hole of a kitchen for a morsel to calm my nerves... only to face my mother.

"Zelda, Zelda, Zelda," she'd chide as she inhaled caffeine laced with scotch, lit another Marlboro, and disappeared down the hall into her paint studio. "The sun is out. The birds are singing," she'd holler. "If you miss the school bus, I am not, I repeat, *not* driving you. You'll just have to stay home."

As I knew this to be true, I simply retired to my bedroom with a bowl of milk-drenched Raisin Bran where I read my favorite depressed Beat poet-turned-folksinger while eating a box of milk-dunked Saltines and planning my life as a famous person so as to ensure that the entire eighth grade would rue the day they called me Stinky Pinky. (The stinky part I have already explained; "pinky" referred to my tendency to turn various shades of puce when I am fearful or humiliated.)

For the next few hours I alternately read and sang a song/poem called "Dusty Rose." I also ate a box of butter cookies, two bananas, a can of cashews, and a bag of potato chips. I felt so sick and disgusted that after I finished the chips, I swore I would never eat again. I thought about throwing up, but the idea turned my stomach. I thought about swallowing a bottle of my mother's antidepressant pills, but that seemed extreme. I thought about asking for help, but I wasn't sure who to ask.

"Zelda!" shrieked my mother from her studio. "Can you bring my cigarettes?"

I ignored her and thought about crying. I hadn't cried since I don't know when. The Beat poets talked a lot about wailing and howling, so I thought I'd give that a try.

"Zelda!" bellowed my mother. "What in God's name is that noise? I need my cigarettes!"

Since howling felt forced and it didn't make me happy, I walked into my mother's room, picked up a carton of Marlboros, and took it to her studio.

"It's about time," she said, flinging red paint at a canvas on the floor.

"Isn't it dangerous to smoke around all this paint stuff?" I asked from the doorway.

She snapped her fingers for the smokes. I handed them over, then I stood back, waiting for her to look at me. She didn't.

I suppose I should have gone back to my room, but something held me there. "Mom?" I asked.

But she didn't answer. She ripped open the carton, grabbed a pack of Marlboros, sliced off the top with her putty knife, and pulled out a cigarette, which she lit from the stub of the butt in her teeth. Then she poured half a can of yellow paint into a can of blue. I knew she was drunk, and I knew she'd probably already forgotten that I was there, but something kept me hanging at her door.

"Mom," I repeated. "I'm very fat and I want to die. I can't stop eating, Mom. I don't know what's wrong with me. I eat till I feel sick, and I want to die and never eat again, but then I do. I'm sick in my soul, Mom. I want to throw up or cry or die, but instead I keep eating. Maybe if we could put locks on the kitchen...but I can pick locks, so that wouldn't work. I'm the fattest kid in my class, Mom, and I don't want to go to school anymore. I think I could be an actress though because I can make things up and believe them. Mom, could I take acting lessons so I could become famous instead of going to school?"

My mother pounded the top onto the can of yellow and blue paint and began to shake it. She shook it violently with the cigarette clenched in her teeth. She shook it so hard her face turned red. Then—crash, splat—she passed out on the floor.

I stamped out her burning butt before it could start a fire on the canvas. I checked my mother's pulse. She was fine, just drunk. She'd come to in a little while and continue as she always did. I grabbed a rag and mopped up the pool of paint from where the yellow and blue can had fallen. I stepped over my mother's body, walked back to her bedroom, took all the money out of her wallet, grabbed my Beat poets book, walked two miles to the train station, and boarded the first locomotive to Manhattan.

My father lived and worked somewhere on the Upper East Side and, upon arriving at Grand Central Station, I briefly considered giving him a call. But I knew he would not appreciate the intrusion, so instead I stepped into a taxicab parked on Vanderbilt Avenue. "Vere do you vant to go?" asked the driver in a heavy East Indian accent.

That's when I realized I had neglected to decide. "How about the hotel where all the famous poets and folksingers live?" I suggested, searching for an address in my depressed poets book. Drat, nothing. "The Chelsea Hotel!" I barked, suddenly remembering the new Leonard Cohen song. It was 1975, and, according to Mr. Cohen, everybody with soul lived at the Chelsea. The driver floored the gas, and in no time he was pulling over in front of 222 West 23rd Street.

My favorite poet went by the name of Mike (not his real name, but close enough). He was famous for the aforementioned song/poem "Dusty Rose." He wrote it in the mid-sixties, and in case you're not up on sixties poetry, I'll remind you that it is the one about a girl with buttocks-length auburn hair who longed to be a ballerina but didn't have the body because she was too Rubinesque, so in disappointment she kills herself. You might recall that Mike sang the song in the voice of the mourning lover on the *Ed Sullivan Show*, and that this had led to many interviews and stories that he was writing a great American epic poem. Even though a decade later he had published nothing, photographs of him with his famous baseball cap pulled down over his sunglasses and his shoulders hunched to his ears to maintain anonymity made it into the tabloids. He was known as a reclusive genius, and I was certain he would recognize my inner beauty and star quality.

I paid the taxi driver generously from my mother's stash and I went inside the hotel.

"I would like to see Mike the poet," I announced to the bald man at the reception desk. He chewed on the end of an unlit cigar and turned the page of his *Daily News*. "Excuse me," I repeated, "I am here to see Mike the poet." I had withstood far worse effronteries than this during six years of elementary school and I would not be intimidated. "He's expecting me. Can you tell me his room number?" The bald man spat cigar bits and scowled. "He ain't here."

"Oh," said I, considering my options. "Well, do you mind if I wait?"

The bald man shrugged and pointed to a circle of flea-bitten red and black armchairs on the other side of this lobby that looked like a crazy art gallery.

I hadn't gone to the bathroom since before my food binge and my bladder was bursting. "Excuse me," I said as politely as I could. "Where is the ladies room?"

"Zat what you are?" said the bald man, looking me up and down in a way that made me feel even sicker. "Down the hall to the left."

Trust me, I'm doing you a favor by sparing you the details of the Chelsea Hotel's public bathroom. The only good part was that it was so awful that I believed simply conjuring it when I felt compelled to eat might be an effective diet plan.

After I was done relieving myself as best I could, given the circumstances of the toilet, I went back to the lobby where I waited for two hours and forty-seven minutes until an old woman with matted grey hair, wearing a purple gown that exposed nearly all of her cleavageless pancake breasts sat down.

"Do you have a joint?" she inquired.

I responded that I did not use drugs, but did she happen to know Mike the poet's suite number?

"Mike doesn't live here," she cooed, licking what was left of her front teeth. "Didn't pay his rent. I think he's uptown at the Embassy."

I didn't know which was more upsetting—Mike's absence or the feeling of her fingers twiddling up my thigh. "What embassy?" I demanded, lurching out of the chair.

The woman grinned. She was in dire need of a dental hygienist. "You're making a joke, right?" Then she laughed like a six-pack-a-day alcoholic, hoisted herself out of the chair, and staggered to the elevator.

I was about to give up and return to Grand Central when I heard a voice behind the *Daily News* at the reception desk: "Embassy Hotel. Broadway and Seventieth Street. If you hurry, you can probably catch him before—"

I was out the door and into another taxi speeding to the Upper West Side before he could finish his sentence.

The Embassy Hotel was far worse than the Chelsea. It smelled of stale puke and the man at reception grinned like the wolf in "Little Red Riding Hood."

"I'm here to see Mike the poet," I announced. "He's expecting me."

"My name ees José," said the clerk. "I like beeg legs."

"I have an appointment with Mike the poet," I repeated, displaying my paperback with his picture on the cover. "Can you tell me his room number?" And as I said it, something that looked like a pile of old blankets on the seedy lobby sofa in the corner heaved and groaned.

"Meester Mike," announced José, making a grand gesture to the pile, "your appointment ees here."

Chapter 2

Mike the poet had a bit of a drinking problem. Also a drug problem. And a problem speaking words...which may have had something to do with his lack of literary production for the last decade.

"I lost my muse," he mumbled as he motioned for me to follow him into an elevator that creaked like a dungeon and smelled even worse than the lobby. "Are you my muse?"

I told him I was Zelda and his song/poem "Dusty Rose" made me know that he and I were soul mates.

"Ah," he said, pondering the import of my statement. Then he was silent until the elevator stopped at the sixteenth floor. And as the doors creaked open, he threw up.

"How old are you?" he asked as he fumbled with his door key a few minutes later.

"How about if I help you with that?" I countered, wresting the key out of his shaky hand. I was used to this kind of thing from my mother.

I turned the key in Mike the poet's door and pushed it open against a mountain of laundry and garbage. Mike staggered to the bed and dropped stomach-first on top of a week's worth of newspapers. "I think I may have a job for you," he mumbled into the newsprint before he passed out. And my heart soared.

For the next few hours, I listened to Mike snore as I cleaned the bathroom. Again, I will spare you details. Suffice it to say I acquired a bucket of maid's supplies from a locked closet in the hall and I used them to scour and scrub and polish for most of the night. Since I'd decided to pretend that I wasn't scared, cleaning was a good use of my adrenaline. I was good at pretending, and doing so under precarious—possibly perilous—conditions was excellent preparation for my future career as a famous actress. I smiled pleasantly, the way the easy-going athletic kids did, as I piled whatever could be piled, exposing a path around the bed to a broken armchair with a split seat cushion where I did my best to rest until daylight.

At around six A.M., Mike the poet moaned, and, holding his crotch, he fell off the bed and crawled into the bathroom. I guess he forgot I was there because he neglected to close the door as he peed and pooped and made all manner of noises. So as not to embarrass him when he realized his gaff, I politely stared at the floor, barely able to breathe or to control my excitement about my impending job. Would I play interference with the paparazzi or contribute in some way to whatever top secret manuscript he might be working on since his record-breaking appearance on Ed Sullivan?

"Who the hell are you?" he demanded from the entrance to the bathroom. His pants were down around his ankles, and although it was my first time seeing an in-person naked man, I remained poised.

"My name is Zelda, and I am ready to help in whatever way you require," I answered. "Might I suggest a clean pair of pants before we discuss your manuscripts?" And I offered him blue jeans from the stack I'd folded at three A.M.

"Shit," said Mike the poet, slamming the bathroom door in my face, and a moment later I heard the shower.

I was very hungry, so I wrote a note in my best script, took his penny jar and the five dollars I'd found in the pocket of the clean blue jeans, and tiptoed out to find the nearest fruit and vegetable market with a selection of cookies and breadstuffs.

The streets of New York City are never quiet, but that morning I discovered that six A.M. is my favorite time. You can walk without being bumped—which is a plus if you are afraid or hate everyone. The vegetable and fruit markets are open but slow moving. And there is lots of spare change in the gutters, dropped by night revelers as they fell, *intoxicé*, out of taxicabs.

(In the years that followed, I found several cash-packed wallets, and had I been a less honest person, willing to advance from invention to the popular crime of identity theft, I don't mind admitting that I might now be an independently wealthy lady living in Switzerland. But I digress.)

The morning after the night of contemplating my new life as an assistant to one of the most renowned poet/songwriters of our time, I was not only extremely hungry, but in dire need of a toilet.

So I made it only one block east to a seedy market on Columbus Avenue with bruised fruit and expired cookie packages. I wanted to buy Mike the poet sweet fruit and cut it into perfect triangles served on a fine china plate with crackers—although I had not seen plates, fine or otherwise, anywhere in that rat hole of a hotel room. I bought napkins and two red delicious apples which I refused to pay for until they were polished clean by the sullen Korean cashier with great sleep bags under his eyes. Then I loaded up on week-expired cellophane packages of cheese and peanut butter sandwich crackers, dumped Mike's penny jar on the counter, and slipped into the employees only bathroom as the Korean cursed and counted. The idea that the world's greatest poet/songwriter was undernourished was untenable, and I could not wait to feed him.

My stomach was making a terrible noise as I stepped into the Embassy elevator, so I consumed several of the cheese and peanut butter sandwich crackers on the way up to the sixteenth floor.

In addition to Mike the poet's money, I had also borrowed the room key, so when I got to 16D, I quietly let myself in, calling, "Mike, it's Zelda," so as not to startle him.

To my surprise, Mike the poet was dressed, sitting upright on the chair I'd slept in, primly eating Rice Crispies out of a milk-filled plastic bag with a small silver spoon. "Hi," he said as if he'd been expecting me. "Thanks for cleaning up. Sorry if I shocked you with my dick."

"I brought you cheese and peanut butter snack sandwiches," I replied.

Sticking the spoon into the bag, he reached for my sack. "You're wonderful. Give 'em here."

"Also apples," I said, handing him the sack.

"You will be the mother of my children," he announced, pulling out a red delicious apple and biting off half.

I am not fond of children, and even at age fourteen, I knew I would not spawn. Nevertheless, I was swept away by the fervor of his declaration.

Chapter 3

When Mike the poet learned my age, he said it would be best if we did not copulate—although I think it was really because of my weight; I was not that much younger than several of the girls who stayed with us during the three months that I was his assistant. Mike the poet called them his "mini-muses" and said he needed copulation at least once a day in order to write. To my knowledge, the only thing he produced were weekly coffee-stained scribbled notes, which I dutifully delivered to José the desk clerk, about his soon-to-be-received book royalties and, the requisite tardy payment of his rent.

Mike the poet's favorite mini-muse was named Matilda. She had wispy blonde hair that she constantly tugged, a baby-doll face, and bruised arms under her long-sleeved lace blouses. She was very nice even though she liked to say "ta-ta" and pretend she was English instead of from the suburbs like me. When she or the other mini-muses were with Mike the poet, he slapped a magnetized plastic "Detour" sign on our door, and I knew to go to the library, or the McDonalds on Amsterdam Avenue where I would order a double-size burger and eat very slowly.

We didn't have a TV, so at night, Mike the poet would tell me stories about his appearance on Ed Sullivan—how he'd sold a million records and books afterward and how he would have won the Pulitzer if only his ex hadn't had him arrested. Apparently after a night of mutual heavy drinking and copulation, he'd merely defended himself from her windmill slaps, inadvertently knocking her out. To this day, he said, she had not recanted her ridiculous accusation that not only was he an abuser, but he'd plagiarized "Dusty Rose" from an unpublished poem of hers. She had never challenged his copyright—ergo, he received uncontested royalties—and *that*, said Mike the poet, should have proved his innocence. But alas, the Pulitzer committee—a bunch of arrogant asses—had ignored him. And boy would they be embarrassed when he won his MacArthur Genius Award.

Mike the poet was very nice to me. He never asked where I was from or where my parents were. He gave me a place to sleep, even if it was a lumpy armchair. And he paid for my food with the money I took from his pockets.

I kept the room clean, and I typed a résumé for him on the hotel's Olivetti one night when I was covering for José who was visiting the prostitutes on the second floor. In exchange for my services, José "forgot" about several weeks' rent, so everybody benefited.

The résumé looked awfully good due to my fanatically neat typing and Mike the poet's Ivy League education and first job as protégé to the founder of a prestigious poetry journal. Also, when he was sober and showered, Mike the poet had an arresting masculine appearance. And the more I told him how wonderful he looked, the more he showered. This proved serendipitous, as he made quite an acceptable impression when, three months after I moved in, an old friend of the prestigious poetry journal founder called out of the blue and asked if Mike the poet would like to be editor-in-chief of a new, edgy, downtown version of the old prestigious poetry journal. Of course, Mike the poet accepted, but I only found out when, after five hours in McDonalds waiting for the "Detour" sign to come down, I asked José if he knew who was in the room with Mike.

"Oh, Mike, he gone," said José, smiling to display his gold caps. "He take hees things six hour ago. Say you pay da rent. Ees due yesterday."

I tried calling Mike the poet at his new office to suggest that he not only pay the rent but consider giving me a stipend for all the work I had done as his assistant, but he never returned my messages.

And that was how I ended up living with Matilda, the baby-doll-faced heroin addict, and being introduced to the world of animal rights.

Chapter 4

"People who experiment on animals should be put to death by hanging or firing squad!" yelled a swarthy, triple-chinned woman, raising her fist and bringing it down hard on the podium.

Although I had never had a pet and I took great pains to conceal my deathly fear of mice, I was intrigued. Before getting addicted to heroin, Matilda had been a pre-med student at New York University with an interest in neurology. That ended after one day in a teaching lab where monkeys with severed sensory nerves housed in body-size cages were being studied. It was assumed that stroke victims with such nerve damage could no longer use arms and legs, although their motor nerves were still intact. Matilda's job was to taunt the starving animals with bananas on a stick to see if they would use limbs they could no longer feel if their working limbs were bound against their sides.

I tried to make sense of this. "Why didn't they just use real stroke victims who already had the problem?"

Matilda shrugged. "Probably 'cause they couldn't keep them in cages."

Disgusted by the torture, she'd said "ta-ta" to the lab, quit college, and moved back home.

After Mike the poet disappeared, Matilda said I could live with her in the co-op studio apartment two blocks from the Embassy Hotel that her parents had bought for her after she'd taken up heroin and they'd kicked her out of the house.

"You can have the futon," she told me, pulling on her wispy hair as if she were trying to stretch it. "There's room in my closet for your stuff, but that's where I grow my weed, so be a dear and don't crush it when you put away your shoes."

For a drug addict, Matilda was very neat, which was a relief after Mike the poet.

"Also, you'd better start looking for your own place because as soon as the money for the commune comes through, I'm saying 'ta-ta.' Also, one house rule: no animal products in the fridge. If you must eat cow, keep it out of my flat."

During the day, Matilda visited with other drug addicts to plan their organic farm commune, and I got a job sweeping floors and stacking canned goods at the nasty Korean deli where I'd bought the peanut butter and cheese sandwich snack crackers. My boss did not speak English, so he never asked how old I was, and he paid me in cash and as many expired breadstuff goods as I could carry. One night a week I took a free acting class with Matilda's ex-boyfriend, a directing student at NYU's theatre school. And the other nights, Matilda and I went to free concerts and animal rights meetings where she distributed fund-raising fliers for her farm.

We were at one such meeting the night the swarthy, triple-chinned woman who wanted to shoot people almost broke the podium. "Oh my God! Oh my God!" she wailed, cradling her swelling hand to her enormous bosom. The audience was too revved up about animal torturers to notice her injury, so they didn't immediately hear the gentleman in the back yelling, "I'm a doctor! Let me through!" It took a while, but finally he elbowed his way to the

podium, yanked the woman's hand out of her bosom, and pro-
nounced it broken. Then he looked at the crowd and, pulling his
thin lips into a weird smile that was not apparent anywhere else on
his face, he said, "Tee hee."

As the crowd quieted, confused by his behavior, he began to
explain. "Actually, I'm a Ph.D." He crumpled the woman's notes
into balls and tossed them at the first row of activists. "My name is
Seth." His tight mouth now matched his steely eyes. "These meetings are a joke. I've been coming for three months, and I'm sick of
talk." The crowd stilled as Seth scanned left to right and back again.
Then turning to the woman with the broken hand, he said, "I'd get
to an emergency room if I were you," and she skedaddled. "All right
then," said Seth to nobody in particular, "I say it's time we took
action. Are you with me? Are you ready to act? Are you willing to
make a statement?" And the crowd went wild.

As I mentioned, I have a severe mouse phobia, but that did not
stop me from going with the others to break into the lab. I decided
to use the adventure as an acting exercise—acting as if I was not
scared out of my wits. It would be excellent preparation for dealing
with my inevitable stage fright when I had my first starring role on
Broadway.

Much to our surprise, gaining access to the Eastside University
Hospital was not difficult. Matilda had worn her Marilyn Monroe
wig and was using it to flirt with the guard while I, Seth, and a
bony raw-foods vegetarian named Stewart stepped into the elevator. At Seth's direction, we had dressed in business attire—I in
a nondescript black muumuu that Matilda had swiped from her

grandmother who really was English and lived in a luxury co-op on the Upper East Side. Seth had given each of us an official looking ID badge, which we waved at the guard as we motioned to Matilda. "There's always one slowpoke," laughed Seth, impatiently tapping his briefcase full of rescue paraphernalia and frowning with his best "I'm a Ph.D." look of gravitas. The guard smiled; I nodded congenially, playing the part of a worldly graduate student with a trust fund; and Matilda said "ta-ta" to the guard and joined us in the elevator.

The thirty-second floor looked like my junior high school with its concrete block walls and grey linoleum floors lit by flickering fluorescent tubes. Seth had instructed us to walk with purpose; no talking. At his direction, we marched to room 48D and grouped in front of the blue steel door. Seth pulled an enormous key ring out of his pocket and searched for the master. For our own protection, he had not told us how he had procured a master key, and nobody asked.

"Like we planned," he said. And as he clicked open the bolt lock, we were met with an explosion of twittering and twerps—like a flock of birds, but less happy—coming from wall-to-wall cages on top of cages on top of counters.

The reason for my mouse phobia has to do with an incident when I was almost five—before my father moved to New York City, never to be seen again, and my mother became a full-time drunk. I was lying in bed, thinking about how when I grew up, I would have my own home. A little house with doors and windows that shut tight, and if my mother knocked and I didn't want to answer, I wouldn't. And if my father forgot about my birthday, it wouldn't matter because my little house had one room that was nothing but toys—dolls the size of real children that would play with me whenever I wanted—not like the mean children in kindergarten who called me stinky fatty and wouldn't let me on the swings, and if I did wangle a seat, would refuse to push me and ran away. This little house would be my home, just the way I wanted, and just as I was thinking this, a dark thing skittered across my bed. I had seen mice in the backyard and in the playground at school, and I'd never felt afraid. But having one on my bed, interrupting my perfect little house fantasy—well, it nearly sent my almost-five-year-old heart into apoplexy, and I've never been able to look at a mouse without a full-body panic attack. So standing in a lab full of the twittering creatures was unnerving.

As Seth, Stewart, and Matilda rushed cage to cage, pulling the squirming things out by their tails and dropping them into burlap sacks with air holes, I froze.

"Whatza matter?" hissed Stewart in a loud stage whisper. "Move your fat ass! And for God's sake, don't you ever shower?"

I do not react well to pressure, so perhaps I overcompensated in my attempt to accommodate Stewart and save the abused rodents. I grabbed the closest cage, intending to pour its inmates into my burlap sack without physical contact, but I hadn't anticipated their athleticism. No sooner had I tipped the cage, unlatching the door, than ten thousand shrieking mice exploded onto the linoleum, scampering every which way. (I later learned that it had been my misfortune to choose the one cage housing an experiment on the emotional implications of overcrowding.)

"What the—!" gasped Stewart, staring at the floor.

"Holy shit!" screamed Matilda. "No, no, I hate mice!"

"For crying out loud," bellowed Seth, falling on his behind in his attempt to avoid stepping on the creatures.

In shock, I dropped the whole cage and fell backwards against the wall—apparently triggering an alarm, because a couple of minutes later, a battalion of security guards burst in on the four of us, on hands and knees trying to herd the terrified rodents into the sacks.

"Shit!" was all the head guard said before he started stamping, and then it was a free for all.

"No!" screamed Seth, Matilda, and Stewart, flinging themselves on the floor, squashing more mice.

"Shit!" bellowed the guards, swinging their night sticks at the three of them, bloodying heads and breaking fingers.

"No," I tried to say, but it came out as a strangled cry as a guard wrestled me to the ground, jerking my hands behind my back.

By the time it was over, it was a mouse holocaust with squashed and bloodied bodies littering the floors and counters and over-turned cages.

Handcuffed and splattered in mouse guts, we were herded into the elevator, and I wondered if Matilda's grandmother would want her muumuu back. If not, could a good dry cleaner remove the damage and my fear stink? I needed clothes; I'd been wearing noth-ing but the same over-sized jeans and peasant blouse I'd left my house in three and a half months ago.

Chapter 5

In the years that followed, I lost track of Matilda, gave up my animal rights work, and significantly expanded my wardrobe—having developed a talent for spotting gently worn, plus-size, thrift-store gems. By 1982 my closet was bursting with bright dresses and long skirts, cardigans and capes and theatrical costumes, along with a more sedate section of nondescript office wear that I longed to get rid of. I could feel it in my bones. It was time for a change: After six years of temp work to pay for my own tiny apartment and my no-longer-free acting classes with Matilda's ex-boyfriend; after a string of successful performances as all manner of creatures and sentient inanimate objects in the ex-boyfriend's experimental avant-garde showcase (no pay) theatre productions; after acting daily in this adventure called life, I just knew I was ready for Broadway. I had passion and moxie, and it was merely bad luck that I was not cute and dimply and ten years younger, but Lord knows I was street smart. So when I heard they were looking for a tough kid for the Broadway production of *Annie*, I decided to give it my best shot.

"I am not a singer," I explained to the producer, "but I have taken two tap lessons, and, as they say in the business, 'I move well.'" To demonstrate, I did several *pirouettes* along with a series of *grande jettés* across his chambers.

Unfortunately, he had not been expecting my spontaneous *pas de Basque* or, for that matter, my appearance. And here I must admit that I had perpetrated a slight deception in order to gain entry. You see, despite my years of training and on-stage exercise of the *métier* of acting, I was not a member of that effete clique of theatrical snobs known as Actors' Equity Association, and therefore was denied my deserved chance to share my talents with those in a position to pay me a living wage. Ergo, I had entered the offices of Mr. Morris Lerner (not his real name) under the guise of delivering a large pastrami on rye and one small Diet Pepsi which I had managed to wrest from the abnormally strong grip of a wiry delicatessen delivery boy named Juan. (In my defense, I did promise Juan ten dollars on my exit, and, as you will soon see, it was not my fault that we never managed to rendezvous.)

As Mr. Lerner reached for his wallet to pay me, I launched into my monologue *sans* song, *avec* pirouettes, and it was just my bad luck that he was a collector of priceless antique porcelains. I offered to reimburse him for the damage out of my meager temp secretary salary, but the man was irrational.

To make a long story short, I was summarily escorted to the street, bypassing Juan who was waiting for me in the broom closet next to the elevator. My escorts were two thugs who years later appeared in bit parts in several films by that over-rated misogynist Martin Scorsese, and unfortunately they grabbed all of my eight-by-ten glossy actor's headshots. Not only were said photos circulated to the other producers on Broadway, but they were plastered on the cash registers of so many local delicatessens that I was blackballed into the obscurity of Matilda's ex-boyfriend's off-off-Broadway experimental abominations and Korean vegetable markets.

So is it any wonder that I altered my course and began exploring additional career paths?

Because I have show biz in my DNA, I soon found myself doing props for a small summer theatre in New England run by a man who, had he not been a Jewish homosexual hippie named Rainbow, I might have mistaken for Adolph Hitler.

Chapter 6

"Miss McFigg," he growled, putting his enormous Crayola-colored sneakers up on the milk crates he called a desk, "Miss McFigg, I asked for an Art Deco sofa. What you have given us is a monstrosity. Do you have an explanation?"

Despite the extreme incivility of having to address his treadless soles, I was determined to remain professional. "Mr. Rainbow," I began.

"How many times do I have to tell you, it's simply Rainbow. One word. One name. Like Cher. Why is that so difficult for you?"

"Given that we have no budget for props," I continued, ignoring his ridiculous reference to a woman whose main claim to fame was her belly button, "due to the fact that I am reduced to borrowing furniture from the local boutique, I thought you would be pleased that I was able to obtain a slightly used Castro Convertible for the mere price of a mention in our photocopied programs."

Mr. Rainbow was not happy, and quite frankly he frightened me. As I have mentioned, when I am frightened, I become not only stinky but clumsy. Add to that my light-headedness due to the fact that for two days I had eaten nothing but one six-ounce can of water-based Chicken of the Sea tuna and four bagels in an attempt to lose a few pounds, and I'm afraid I accidentally dropped the Art Deco vase I was holding onto his milk crates. "Miss McFigg!" he screamed, further unnerving me so that I leaned into the life-size nude papier-mâché reproduction of the Venus de Milo that was going to be featured in our next production, *Pygmalion and Galatea, an Original Mythological Comedy*, a blank verse play in three acts by Sir W. S. Gilbert. And that's how my career doing props for a small New England theatre came to an end.

Chapter 7

I liked New England. The quaint village shoppes, the neat little houses with pristine picket fences, the polite repartee between local folk. So I decided to stay. When I was fired from the summer theatre, I was also evicted from the concentration camp they called staff housing, so my first order of business was to find a place to live. You would think a tidy single lady with no pets and a passion for *les beaux mots* would have no problem, but alas, the polite New England folk had their share of bias when it came to artistes. As I mentioned, I had taken up tap dancing shortly before leaving off-off-Broadway, and I required a home where other residents would not mind several short periods of rhythmic practice. Finally, I managed to procure just the right ground floor apartment in the house of one Mrs. Etta Mendelson, a severely anorexic wisp of a woman who needed grounding and could not hear. Our mutually compatible disabilities—my weight, her deafness—worked quite well for both of us...until the fire.

The problem began with baseball. Although I have never watched a whole game, I feel entitled to my opinion. And my opinion is that baseball is a puerile pastime practiced by overpaid boys who would do better to cut to the chase and sell insurance. However, despite its inanity, baseball does have one of the preeminent anthems of athletics. Namely "Take Me Out to the Ball Game," with its perfect tempo for the practice of slow-motion shuffle-ball-changes.

I don't mind saying that following my termination as prop mistress of the small summer theatre, I fell into a state of ennui. To be honest, ennui does not do justice to my emotional abyss. By the end of my first week at Mrs. Mendelson's, I was in need of antidepressant medications. Unfortunately, such aids did not fit into the budget of an unemployed artiste, so as an alternative, I decided to activate my endorphins with twenty minutes of slow-motion waltz clog. As accompaniment, I put on the aforementioned recording, and I'm amazed to admit that until that moment, I had never seriously considered the gravitas of the lyrics:

> *Take me out to the ball game,*
> *Take me out with the crowd.*
> *Buy me some peanuts and Cracker Jack,*
> *I don't care if I never get back . . .*

I ask you, dear reader, to contemplate these words, and perhaps you will understand how they sounded to a desperately hungry person who had not only lost her job, but her option to go back to New York City due to a nasty eviction from her off-off-Broadway apartment—an event I fear I have forgotten to mention.

You see, in a fit of hunger-induced bad judgment whilst completely out of cash after being blackballed by my temp secretarial agency due to a misunderstanding about borrowed office supplies, I seem to have swiped one yellow delicious apple from my former place of employ, the nasty neighborhood Korean market. To make a somewhat dreary epic short, my bail and the exorbitant fine ren-

dered me incapable of paying rent, and it was in this penniless state
that I'd fled to New England and my fleeting job as prop mistress
to the Jewish homosexual of questionable mental health.

With this background, I'm sure you can relate to my feelings,
waltz-clogging to a song about happy people enjoying the company
of others while eating caramel-covered snacks when I was reduced
to eating Chicken of the Sea in a one-room hovel owned by a deaf
woman with a bird—well, it threw me into a depression I scarcely
know how to describe. So when I suddenly heard Mrs. Mendelson's
bird yelling, "Let me out! Let me out!" I don't have to tell you, I
could relate.

I've never understood the infantilizing of animals, and even
worse, the incarceration of one that is meant to be flying amongst
the treetops eating bugs. So when I heard Barnard—Mrs. Mendelson named the creature after her late husband, whose voice
the bird apparently mimicked perfectly; although, being deaf and
near death from anorexia (which, I must admit, I aspired to, but I
lacked the discipline), how could the old woman have known? But
I digress. When Barnard screamed "Let me out!" I simply could
not deny him.

Mrs. Mendelson was doing errands in town and had left the poor
creature in an eight-by-five-foot prison. My only intention when I
headed up the impossibly rickety steps to the second floor, was to
allow the animal the modicum of freedom Mrs. Mendelson herself
permitted him when she was home.

I let myself in with a bobby pin—an invaluable talent, alluded
to earlier, that I seem to have been born with—and to say I was
appalled is an understatement.

In my opinion, sloppy people should not be allowed to have pets,
and certainly not birds who would never choose to live in such
conditions. Have you ever seen a sloppy forest?

I looked through several of Mrs. M's magazines—ten years or older—I believe the psychiatric term is hoarding. Then I made my way around the stacks of boxes and piles of unlaundered undergarments to the bedroom where Barnard was imprisoned. "Lemme out, fatty!" he bellowed in the late Mr. Mendelson's thick Bronx accent.

Despite my enjoyment of winged creatures in nature—and I do love those Public Television specials—I was rather unnerved by the sight of this flapping red caldron of fury glaring at me with vicious yellow eyes and addressing me so rudely. As I mentioned, fear seems to affect my motor skills, and to make matters worse, I was wearing my patent-leather Mary Jane tap shoes whose soles were particularly slick due to my lack of recent practice. As I leaned forward over the mountain of rags and boxes that surrounded the cage, I seem to have lost my footing. At which point, the brute screamed, "Fatty, fatty, fatty!" further disorienting me. And as I and the cage toppled toward the window, my only thought was to avoid shattering the glass. Which is why I grabbed for the nearest source of support. A floor-sized halogen lamp—switched on in order to keep the room tropically warm, Mrs. Mendelson later explained to the fire department.

As a formerly homeless person myself, I deeply regret my actions that led to the incineration of the overstuffed hovel Mrs. Mendelson called home, and I wrote a statement to that effect and accepted the lien on all future earnings. But between you and me, there is one thing that I do not have the least remorse about: As I crawled through the flames on my stomach, I saw Barnard. It seems that the crash unlocked his cell, and as he flew out the shattered window, I swear he winked at me.

Needless to say, my reputation was soiled in the small New England town, and the polite local folk dealt with it by shunning me. Icy smiles and speedy exits met my entreaties to converse and explain the situation. So posthaste and predawn I vacated my emergency shelter at the Crappy Motel (not its real name), leaving an IOU along with an extremely apologetic note, and I used my remaining funds to purchase a bus ticket to the northern regions where talk was minimal, housing much cheaper, and the main industries were snowmobiles and moose.

Chapter 8

Despite my disorientation at landing in the Vermont tundra, I assured the realtor of my ability to pay rent just as soon as I received my first paycheck and I quickly procured housing—a minuscule but darling gate cabin at the entrée to the unoccupied estate of the Montavaldo family, who only migrated north at the peak of summer and no doubt had purchased their ten acres with laundered funds from nefarious endeavors. Unfortunately, I soon learned that job opportunities for ex-temp/ex-thespian/ex-prop mistress persons were few, so, ignoring my antipathy for children, I gratefully accepted the post of part-time hall monitor in the Moose Country Middle School System, and was near-deaf and cross-eyed from urchin noise when, a few weeks into my tenure, Mrs. Freeman, the ninety-year-old English teacher, dropped dead mid-sentence about Mr. Jack London's remarkable "law of club and fang," and I stepped in to quell the roar.

Understand that I now embodied the law of club and fang, having landed in the tundra after a failed artistic career, a confusing sequence of domicile displacements, seven and one-half years of sleep problems due to mouse nightmares following my unfortunate foray into the world of animal rights activism, and a brutal bus ride during which I made a personal commitment to turn my life around, to be an upstanding citizen, and to say "yes" to whatever opportunities came my way. So of course I answered "Yes!" to all questions regarding my fitness to replace Mrs. Freeman. "Yes!" to my requisite credentials and experience teaching English in New York City schools. "Yes!" I assured Principal Appleton, "I know the state requirements and can pick up where Mrs. Freeman left off. No problem!" I did not think about consequences should my ruse be discovered. Survival was my sole concern.

Although I was a mere twenty-one years of age, my discomfiture, exhaustion, and weight gave me a mature appearance, and as I did my ablutions the morning of my professorial debut, I was actually grateful for my matronly jowls and general bulk. Perhaps they would pass for muscle and certitude—if not with the juvies, hopefully with their parents and the rest of the faculty, some of whom had raised an eyebrow at the fast-tracking of my hire.

I had a vague idea of what a seventh grade English teacher did from my vague memory of my last school experience. Also, I had heard the late Mrs. Freeman's classes from my hall monitor post, so I was not without preparation. To tell you the truth, I had rather enjoyed her discussions of Mr. London's *The Call of the Wild*. I was so intrigued that I'd borrowed the book from the Moose Country Public Library and read it to the end. Perhaps it was my enthusiasm for the glorification of the primitive and visceral fight for survival, as demonstrated by Mr. London's protagonist, Buck the dog, which convinced Principal Appleton that I was the one for the job. I do not know. But suffice it to say, I needed work and was determined to turn over a new leaf by becoming a model Moose Country citizen teacher. (To that end, I surreptitiously returned my *Complete Works of Jack London* to the Moose Country Library shelf until I had procured a proper library card, at which point I legally borrowed the book—forever.)

You see, I identify with outlaws, and perhaps this is the reason I resonated with Mr. London's Buck the dog. And perhaps for this reason also I might have been a tad over-dramatic in my first reading in front of the Moose Country juvies. In case you are interested, this is the passage I chose for my foray into seventh grade academia (it involves the theft of a bit of fish):

> *This first theft marked Buck as fit to survive in the hostile Northland environment. It marked his adaptability, his capacity to adjust himself to changing conditions, the lack of which would have meant swift and terrible death. It marked, further, the decay or going to pieces of his moral nature, a vain thing and a handicap in the ruthless struggle for existence. It was all well enough in the Southland, under the law of love and fellowship, to respect private property and personal feelings; but in the Northland, under the law of club and fang, whoso took such things into account was a fool, and in so far as he observed them he would fail to prosper.*

"Hello, class. My name is Miss McFigg," I announced to thirty stunned faces. My dramatic flare was no doubt a new experience for this group of moose-hunting heathens. "I will be teaching this class for the remainder of the term, and as I have a background as a thespian in the New York theatre, I will be concentrating on the meaning of *The Call of the Wild* by Mr. Jack London in terms of what it means to the play within the play that composites our individual life meaning so as to enhance our appreciation, while building on Mrs. Freeman's discussion of plot, setting, and vocabulary."

"Miss McFigg," interrupted a bullish looking boy in the back row, and without waiting for me to acknowledge him, he announced that *The Call of the Wild* was his grandfather's favorite story and he already appreciated it, so he could relate to my enthusiasm—at which the classroom erupted with catcalls and boos and a fusillade of spitballs. I deduced from this that the boy was the class scapegoat, and I instantly vowed to be his mentor and savior.

Apparently the boy's grandfather was well-known as the town drunk, and he was an Indian. The boy's name was Donny Sherman, and due to our mutual weight problems, I felt an instant camaraderie.

"Donny," said I with all the compassion I could exude, "I'm so pleased that you are familiar with this text. In that case, you will be my special student, perhaps suggesting topics for discussion and homework assignments."

In my defense, I was trying to make Donny feel valued, so I was caught off-guard by the vocal uproar. Donny, however, seemed strangely oblivious. He sat back in his chair, gazing at me with a knowing look, allowing the ridicule and raspberries to waft over him like a gentle breeze.

Chapter 9

I no longer remember the other classes I taught that first day, but nearly three decades hence, I still vividly recall my state by the time the dismissal bell shrilled, releasing the Moose Country inmates into the hinterland. In an attempt to self-soothe, I decided to tidy. I began by washing down the chalkboard in precise top to bottom strokes. I had believed my theatrical experience was adequate preparation to lecture a roomful of seventh graders, but, alas, I had underestimated the degenerate nature of my audience. "Miss McFigg," said a polite voice, startling me out of my rumination.

"Oh," said I. "Donny. Yes, what can I do for you?" Perhaps I should have been more stand-offish, but the truth is I was drawn to the boy. He was taller than I—in a comforting, dare I say, fatherly kind of way—and almost as heavy, but he seemed comfortable. Unusual for one so young, and I was curious to know the source of his maturity.

"Miss McFigg," he said, "I'm sorry if I scared you. I just wanted to say I really liked the way you read *The Call of the Wild* today."

"Oh," I said, blushing slightly, and, dreading the usual accompanying genetically determined stink, I glued my arms to my sides as well as a severely overweight lady can, and, in the process, dropped my chalk sponge.

"Allow me," said Donny, leaning over to pick it up and emitting the very odor I was trying to avoid. Had he been a bit closer to my age ... but I banished the thought. I was his *teacher*, and I would act professionally. "Miss McFigg," he continued, resting the soggy sponge on the chalk tray, "the kids here can be sort of rough. I hope they didn't get to you with all the 'fatty' comments and noises and stuff. They say that stuff to me all the time. I know it can be harsh."

"Oh, Donny," I said, repressing a swoon.

Maybe it was the fact that I was back in school—a place I'd fled at age fourteen—so in some way it felt like I'd ricocheted back in time with a chance for a do-over. Or maybe it was this boy's kind voice and gentlemanly manner. But suddenly I was overcome by an overwhelming urge to hug him, so I busied my hands by searching through my purse.

"Miss McFigg," said Donny, but I silenced him with a professional educator's touch to his ever-so-soft shoulder.

Perhaps it was physical contact after so many years of none. Or perhaps it was meeting a kindred soul in the middle of the tundra—a boy with the same flayed posture as mine because of our inability to put our legs together or truly flatten our arms to our sides. Looking at this male mirror image of my struggles and heartache, I felt as if I would come apart if he said another word.

"Donny, I have something to tell you," I said, with no idea what that might be. "Would you like a soap?" And out of my purse, I withdrew one of my antibacterial bars for my genetically determined body odor disorder.

Donny Sherman was an orphan. His mother, an Abenaki Indian, had died at age fourteen—a difficult age, it would seem—during Donny's birth. She'd never told anybody who had raped her, so

Donny's father was unknown. Donny lived with his grandfather, a former tracker, now full-time alcoholic surviving on a stipend from his tribal council. The boy and his grandfather shared two rooms with no indoor plumbing and, due to his grandfather's forgetfulness, Donny had started school late and was a year older than the rest of his class. He was very nice about the soap, accepting it respectfully and placing it in the pocket of his battered Army jacket. He told me that nobody knew what they were doing in this school, so if I wanted to forget about *The Call of the Wild* and go on to some other books—any books that I fancied—it would be fine. Nobody read them anyway, so I should just fill out the requisition forms, which would get lost in the principal's office. All I had to do was promote everyone at the end of the year, and nobody would ask any questions. Donny aspired to a career as a trendsetter, and by the way, had I met John Belushi?

Chapter 10

Although my minuscule gate cabin at the entrée to the Montavaldo estate was only one room right on the road—with no actual gate— it was lovely. There was no need for a gate as my road was a dead end; it was very quiet, and I had everything I needed because the Montavaldos used the cabin as a warehouse for their children's out-grown furniture and sundries. I slept comfortably on two child-size single beds pushed together, covered by one blue and purple and yellow and orange butterfly quilt. I had lost most of my clothes in Mrs. Mendelson's fire, so I stored my meager wardrobe in a small maple armoire. Since there was no TV, for my evening's entertain-ment, I chose from a selection of children's picture books, young adult novels, and miscellaneous how-to paperbacks and short story anthologies that I found under a load of mildewed towels in a Native American sweetgrass basket on the floor in the bathroom.

Donny Sherman had said that nobody would remember any-thing I said, so not to worry about making good on promises or consistency of discussion topics from one day to the next. I had never read *Charlotte's Web*, and since it was at the top of the sweet-grass basket and short enough to finish in one sitting, I chose it.

Also, it continued the animal motif begun by *The Call of the Wild*, satisfying my own need for connective thread.

"All right, class, will you please step down from your desks and windowsills?" I implored my third period class. "Be seated please!" But everyone but Donny ignored me.

My first period homeroom had gone rather well, even though the children had switched seats and caused havoc with roll call, answering with such phrases as "in person" and "in the flesh" and "deceased." Second period was study hall, which I used to go over my *Charlotte's Web* notes, so I was not bothered by the throwing of chairs and overturning of desks. But third period was show time, and I would not abide disruption of my production. What to do, I wondered. And suddenly I was hit by a thespian's inspiration.

"Tee hee," said I, pretending to be Seth, the mouse liberator, and one-handedly catching a thrown paper ball. Then I pulled my lips into a weird smile, hoping to scare the children quiet. "These classes are a joke," I boomed, tossing the ball at the first row of students. And I glared furiously.

Success. Thirty silent children stared back.

"All right then," I continued, "as yesterday's dramatic reading was so popular, I've decided that today we will all participate in an ensemble presentation of *Charlotte's Web* by the famous author, Mr. E. B. White. How many of you have read this classic novel?"

"Isn't that a kid's book?" said a long-necked girl named Geraldine through a mouthful of chewing gum.

"You will play the goose," I answered, and the class cheered—a good beginning.

"This is stupid," said a skinny boy with big plastic glasses and a perpetual smirk in the back row.

"You will play Templeton the rat," I replied, glaring at him with my most intimidating expression. And I continued assigning parts. I wanted to give Donny the starring role of Wilbur the pig, but I hesitated, fearing the class's reaction. So instead, I made casting a general question. "Who wants to play Wilbur the pig?" I queried, looking at everyone but Donny.

And the class burst into a chant: "Don-ny! Don-ny!"

"I would like to play that part," said Donny, grinning at me.

I had no choice. "Very well," I said. "And I will play the title role of Charlotte the spider, as well as the narrator."

I had spent the previous evening carefully editing the recitation sections by placing Post-its labeled with character names on appropriate pages. Since we only had my copy of the book from the sweetgrass basket, I arranged the children in a rough reading sequence and told them to pass the book among themselves. All went well until we got to the chapter called "Wilbur's Boast."

"I can smell you from here," said the lamb, played by a girl named Peggy who was clearly one of the popular clique. She had a long blonde ponytail and red fingernails. As she spoke her line to Donny/Wilbur, she crinkled her delicate little nose to the others and pointed at Donny. "You're the smelliest creature in the place," she shrieked, and the class went wild.

I attempted to remedy the situation through my narrator lines: "Wilbur hung his head. His eyes grew wet with tears," I read, hoping to elicit empathy in this mob of young sociopaths, but it was hopeless. "Leave Wilbur alone!" I read, letting my own rage out through Charlotte. "He has a perfect right to smell, considering his surroundings. You're no bundle of sweet peas yourself." But I was drowned out by shouts and fart noises.

Donny's face turned a pained and pinched pink, and he hunkered forward wrapping his soft arms around his massive belly. From the way he twisted away from Peggy, I knew he had a crush on her. I knew he felt as if he was being electrocuted, and, worse, if he let it show, it would trigger the class to turn up the current. In an effort to hide, this two-hundred-pound boy turned in on himself, digging his fists into his gut, staring at the floor, his head so bowed that it multiplied his double chins to four.

"Hey, the pig likes Peggy!" yelled the boy with the smirk playing Templeton the rat.

As I felt Donny's anguish in my own flesh, a bomb exploded in my gut. Such cruelty deserved self-righteous anger—an anger that had been brewing since kindergarten, an anger that no adult had offered in my defense when I was in Donny's position. "This must stop!" I roared, and grabbing Templeton's chair, I threw him onto the floor. "Enough! No more! Enough!"

Silence.

"So there!" I said, ignoring the thirty pairs of stunned eyes, and I marched out of the classroom, down the hall to the teachers' restroom, where I stayed until the fourth period bell shrilled, announcing the first wave of lunch.

I was certain that I would be fired, and the inevitability made me brave. Who cares, I told myself. At least I did the right thing. At least that boy would know that one adult on the planet cared and had taken a stand to protect him. If it meant unemployment, so be it. I took my time rinsing my armpits with my antibacterial soap. Then I sat on the toilet to enjoy several Hostess Twinkies that I always carried in my purse for just such emergencies. When I was done, I freshened my face with cold water, applied a new foundation, and checked my lipstick. Then, ten minutes late for my scheduled lunch monitoring duty, I sauntered out of the lounge and down the hall to the cafeteria where I was to rendezvous with Mr. Chuck, the boys' gym and biology teacher, for lunch monitoring orientation.

Fourth period: half of my students had algebra in the classroom next door to mine, and the other half had lunch, so I knew I would have to face them. Although I had no idea what that might involve, I was certain of the final outcome once Mr. Chuck learned that I'd physically abused a student and abandoned my class. I knew he would have to report me to Principal Appleton, and as soon as word spread, nobody in all of Moose Country would hire me, and I'd have to leave my darling gate cabin and move to Canada. As I looked through my change purse for fifty cents to buy a new supply of purse-size snacks from the lunch ladies, I made a mental note to get a passport. I'd never had one, and I wondered if there would be trouble due to my various brushes with the New York City Police Department.

There seemed to be general pandemonium outside the cafeteria. Mr. Chuck, a former Navy man, was yelling at the children to "shape up or ship out," but nobody was listening. In frustration, he tried to herd the urchins toward the walls, but it was useless. The boys were yelling something about a monster, and the girls were shrieking like the mice in the animal lab. "Stop this right now, or it's detention for everyone!" hollered Mr. Chuck.

"There she is! There she is!" shrieked Geraldine, sounding every bit like the goose she'd played in *Charlotte's Web*. She was pointing at me. Then all the children began yelling about me and Donny Sherman, all the while pressing in on Mr. Chuck, backing him into the cafeteria, down the food aisle and into the lunch ladies' check-out desk.

"One at a time!" bellowed Mr. Chuck. "Miss McFigg what? Donny who?"

To my good fortune, my actions were never delineated in the ensuing chaos.

"Donny Sherman is what?" screamed Mr. Chuck, deducing from the intelligible dribs and drabs that something had happened to Donny.

"What's going on here?!" demanded Principal Appleton, elbowing his way through the crowd. "Miss McFigg, what in God's name—"

"Donny Sherman is barricaded in Miss McFigg's classroom holding Peggy Smithson hostage!" declared Templeton the rat, in a voice that belied his small, wiry appearance. In fact, it was a huge voice, and in response, the mob quieted.

"What?" said Principal Appleton, trying to locate the voice.

"Right here," said Templeton in his big voice. "I said Donny Sherman has gone mad and has taken Peggy Smithson hostage."

"Miss McFigg, is this true?" demanded Principal Appleton, glaring at me. "What the blazes is going on here?"

"Miss McFigg is the reason," began Templeton, but he was drowned out by another explosion of shouting as the pressure of the mob overturned the lunch ladies' cooler on top of the check-out desk—once again deflecting attention away from me.

It seems that following my brutalization of Templeton, Donny Sherman decided he'd had enough. Enough bullying. Enough scapegoating. Enough of being everyone's fatty and his grandfather's whipping boy. And using his bulk to his advantage, he'd fallen on Templeton, pinning him to the floor and threatening to break his arms if everyone but Peggy didn't leave the room. Peggy tried to leave with the others as they charged for the door, but being a self-serving and cowardly lot, they'd pushed her back into the room. As soon as it was clear that Peggy had no recourse but to stay, Donny had released Templeton, who had scurried out like the rat he was.

Donny had made no demands, but he'd locked the door from the inside. By the time the whole story was told, the entire Moose

Country Middle School faculty and student body were in the hall outside the cafeteria, and everybody had forgotten about me.

I used the opportunity to pocket several vacuum-packed peanut butter and jelly sandwiches from the overturned cooler, and I munched peacefully as Appleton phoned the Moose Country police. Tomorrow, if I didn't get fired, I would go on a diet. I silently promised this to the universe as I did my best to conjure the Chelsea Hotel bathroom—but it seemed to have lost its bite.

"Come out now and we'll talk about this reasonably," said the Moose Country sheriff through a megaphone. We had all been ordered to evacuate the school. I'm not sure why, since I'd explained to both Appleton and the sheriff that the brouhaha was about a harmless boy with an unreciprocated crush and no weapons. But I believe Moose Country was imploding from years of snow and boredom, and Sheriff Bodwell had decided to use the current drama to show off his new red megaphone. As his deputy cordoned off the students and teachers behind a shiny new yellow police tape, parents began to arrive.

"Young man," said the amplified sheriff, "if you harm the girl, there will be consequences!"

"Oh, for goodness sake," I erupted, but before I could get to the sheriff, the awning window to my classroom cranked open and Donny leaned through the opening, smiling sheepishly. He struggled to get one arm and his head through, but he couldn't fit.

"Some pig," said a man behind me, and quashing my impulse to slug him, I remembered *Charlotte's Web.* That's what Charlotte wrote to save Wilbur: *Some Pig.* And since everybody had believed whatever was in writing, they began to venerate Wilbur.

"Excuse me," said I with all of my thespian training from Matilda the drug addict's ex-boyfriend. "Sheriff Bodwell, as I told you before, Donny is my student. He is a terrific boy. I believe he will talk to me and we can resolve this matter, if only you'll let me—"

"Miss McFigg!" yelled Donny with his head caught in the window opening. "I need to talk to Miss McFigg!"

After several arguments about proper hostage negotiation protocol and whether or not Principal Appleton's secretary, Mrs. Lambert, had ever made a set of keys to the classrooms, and if so, their whereabouts, the sheriff told the deputy to escort me to the window.

The Moose Country Middle School was a one-level red brick octopus of a building whose sprawling tentacles were added willy-nilly as the Moose Country parents procreated. We were standing outside one of the east tentacles which housed my classroom, the math teacher's room, home ec., and the teachers' lounge *avec* restroom. All had identical awning windows that cranked open wide enough to allow the minimum oxygen for consciousness, while prohibiting defenestration to the blacktop three feet below.

"Hi, Donny, what are you doing?" I asked in a conversational tone. I could see Peggy Smithson sitting cross-legged on top of my desk. She was chewing the end of her ponytail and checking her nail polish.

"I'll only talk if *he* leaves," answered Donny, indicating the deputy. I could tell he was saying this to enhance my position, and I played along.

"Certainly, Donny," I replied. "Deputy, would you give us a moment?"

"Yeah, but—"

"Sheriff," I called, "can we please have a little privacy?"

The crowd made an apprehensive "Oh" sound and began to mumble. I liked this and decided to milk the moment, as we say in show business. "Donny says he will only speak to *me*," I declared. "Ergo—"

"All right. All right," said the sheriff through his megaphone. "Phil, give them some space." And the deputy retreated back to the crowd.

"So how is everything?" I asked Donny, gesturing forcefully with my hands in order to look as if I were making demands.

"I'm getting a little hungry," said Donny. "I missed lunch."

"Would you like a vacuum-packed peanut butter and jelly sandwich?" I asked.

"Sure," he answered, and I pulled the last one out of my purse and handed it to him through the window. "Thanks," he said as he unwrapped it.

"How's Peggy doing?" I asked.

"I'm fine," called Peggy from my desktop. "You got anymore sandwiches?"

"Sorry," I said. "So what's all this about?"

"It's really stupid," said Peggy, dejected at my lack of lunch. "I didn't think they'd make such a big deal out of it. I only wanted to miss my algebra test."

"Excuse me?" I said. This was getting confusing.

"I told her she could go whenever she wanted," said Donny. "All's I wanted was to tell her she hurt my feelings. But after I said it, she wouldn't leave. So what do we do now? Are they going to arrest me? I don't want to get Peggy in trouble. Where'd you get this sandwich? It's really stale."

For the sake of the sheriff et al., I pursed my lips as if this were a serious situation. "Why don't you both just come out?" I suggested. "Tell the truth?"

"No way!" yelled Peggy. "My mom will send me to boarding school in Sweden and I'm not missing prom."

I pursed my lips again the way I'd seen actors on police shows do. "I wonder what Charlotte would do in a case like this."

"You need something in writing," said Donny. The boy was a genius.

"Huh?" said Peggy.

"People believe anything that's in writing," said Donny and I in unison.

"Okay, what do you need?" said Peggy, picking up my lined pad like a stenographer. "Anything to get me some lunch."

"A statement of confusion and remorse," said I, after a moment of contemplation. "Something to convey Donny's extreme emotional distress"—a term I'd heard on police shows back when I had a TV. "Something to make this sound like a big misunderstanding. Something that presents Peggy as choosing to stay, out of compassion for her deeply upset classmate."

"Ooo, I like that," said Peggy as she wrote.

"Page 164!" I called, using my photographic memory to locate Charlotte's speech about friendship. "Page 164 of *Charlotte's Web*, the paragraph that begins 'You have been my friend.'"

Instantly, Peggy, a born plagiarist, knew where I was going with this, and she set to work converting Mr. E. B. White's excellent prose into an explanation of why she was holed up in a classroom of the Moose Country Middle School with the fattest boy in town. A few minutes later, with appropriate gravitas, Donny handed me the note and I read her statement to the Moose Country audience:

> "Donny Sherman has been my friend,"
> says Peggy. "That in itself is a tremendous
> thing. I stayed with him because I like
> him. After all, what's a life anyway? We're
> born, we live a little while, we die."

"Oh," gasped the crowd, and I gestured for silence.

> "A girl's life can't help being something of
> a mess. But by helping Donny in his time
> of anguish due to the insensitive remarks
> of his classmates about his weight prob-
> lem and disgusting body odor, by staying
> with my friend in his time of need, per-
> haps I was trying to lift up my life a trifle.
> Heaven knows anyone's life can stand a
> little of that."

"Ah," sighed the crowd with new empathy. And as Principal
Appleton, Mrs. Lambert, and the parents looked at one another in
agreement, I extemporized:

"You see, this is not a case of hostage holding. Donny Sherman
is a terrific boy, a humble boy. He merely needed a friend. This
is a case of one friend standing by another at a time of crisis—as
we all would hope our friends would do. Both of the children are
extremely sorry for the trouble this misunderstanding has caused,
and I hope you can see it in your hearts to forgive them. They
would like to come out now, if they can be assured that you will
not arrest them."

Sheriff Bodwell and Deputy Phil exchanged looks, and Principal
Appleton glared at Mrs. Lambert and mouthed how this whole
thing was her fault. Then Mr. Chuck said something about raging
adolescent hormones, and everybody agreed that if the children
came out and Donny talked to Mrs. Lagerfelt, the guidance counselor and home ec. teacher, no charges would be filed.

Donny and Peggy exited, arms linked. (A nice touch, if I do
say so.) Instantly the adults surrounded Peggy, praising her for her

compassion, and they never noticed that she was carrying the year's algebra tests with answers. Donny, relieved to be out of the spotlight, looked at me across the blacktop and mouthed, "I love you."

Chapter 11

*Asphyxia (suffocation, stoppage of breath-
ing) may accompany any accident causing
unconsciousness or interference with breathing: electric shock, lightning stroke, drowning, drug or chemical poisoning, gas poisoning, smoke inhalation, insufficient oxygen
in confined spaces, injuries, foreign bodies
in the throat, strangulation, hanging, com-
pression and smothering, convulsions, and
cardiac arrest.*

The next part of the all-purpose first aid book that I found in
my sweetgrass basket was a step-by-step guide to mouth-to-mouth
artificial respiration. It seemed like a good subject for young degen-
erates. It had structure, physical activity, and good vocabulary. I
could have the students read, then practice composing their own
instructional essays, thus exercising their logical thinking skills.

Principal Appleton wanted to see me before first period, so I
arrived at the brick octopus early and parked my bicycle, courtesy

of one of the Montavaldo children, in the faculty lot, and chained it to a telephone pole. I was a tad heavy for a child's bike and I made a mental note to ask around for a pump to plump up the tires.

Principal Appleton was also the shop teacher, and his office served for both positions. Mrs. Lambert, his secretary, sat guard in an outer office that looked like the Department of Motor Vehicles. Only her head was visible behind a room-length metal counter facing a wall of faculty mailboxes. My box still had Mrs. Freeman's name label—which would remain for my tenure. They offered to change it after my first twenty-five years, but by then everybody was accustomed to the misnomer and changing it would have been cataclysmic for Mrs. Lambert, who was extremely sensitive about her dyslexia.

"I'm here to see Principal Appleton," I announced, happily swinging my new Montavaldo child's Donald Duck book bag as I peered over the counter.

From her tightly wound black head-top bun to her spastic hands, Mrs. Lambert looked horrified. "Principal Appleton is not here yet," she said with quivering cheeks and no visible movement of her pencil-line mouth. "Do you have an appointment?" Her fingers shook as she examined her calendar. "I don't see an appointment here."

"He told me to meet him here before first period," I said, feeling my bike-induced endorphin exhilaration evaporate as I turned into a frazzled blob. I wasn't even worth a written appointment. Oh my God, I was going to be fired after all. "He told me in the parking lot, after the mishap with—"

"Yes, yes, yes," sputtered Mrs. Lambert. "I understand. Once again Principal Appleton has made my job impossible, scheduling appointments without telling me or noting them on the calendar. I'll write you in. You're welcome. I'm sorry. Take a seat."

I've explained how I react to stress, and to make matters worse, the two collapsible wooden chairs she indicated for me to sit on seemed to be designed for anorexic children or dwarfs. With all my thespian's imagination, I tried to conjure the Chelsea Hotel bathroom, but it was gone. I *would* lose weight. But rather than risk a fat person's catastrophe with my present bulk, I leaned against the wall—triggering the public address system which came on with a blast of earsplitting feedback.

"Oh my goodness, I'm so sorry," I yelled as Mrs. Lambert flailed.

"Turn it off! Turn it off!" she screamed, alternately holding her ears and slapping air. "Please! Please!"

"How? How?" I yelled, unable to find the appropriate switch. There were so many, and each seemed to turn on another bell or siren.

"What the blazes is going on here?!" shouted Principal Appleton, sprinting into the office. "For God's sake!" And as he turned off all the sound systems, he glared at Mrs. Lambert.

"She's here for an appointment," said Mrs. Lambert after silence was restored. "You didn't write it on the calendar."

Ignoring her, Principal Appleton brusquely gestured for me to follow him into the inner office.

Principal Appleton's desk was an ongoing construction that shop students added to during the first class of each new year. "Watch out for the table saw," he warned, directing for me to take a seat. "I must apologize for Mrs. Lambert. She's a charity case you know— the learning disabilities. I don't dare let her go for fear of a lawsuit. Those disabled folks are vicious. Now about yesterday—"

"About that—"

"Excellent crisis management skills."

"Oh," I said. "Oh. Well, for my meager salary as a hall monitor, it's the least I could have—"

"Yes, about that," interrupted Appleton. "A misunderstanding, I assure you."

"Excuse me?"

"Of course you should be given a raise. It was an oversight. Please assure your union that I am well aware that a starting teacher's salary exceeds that of a part-time hall monitor."

"Yes, but—"

"And of course I understand that coming from New York City, you are not a beginner. How about forty dollars a week?"

"You're going to pay me forty dollars a week?" I gasped.

"Certainly not. I meant as an add-on to the base pay. I meant to do this when we hired you, but you and your union must understand the stress—losing Mrs. Freeman so suddenly three weeks into the term. Here's the standard contract. Look it over. By all means, have your union rep examine it. By the rules, tell him. We do things by the rules at Moose Country Middle, and we certainly do not need a reprise of last year's nonsense with Mrs. Lagerfelt. Please just sign the thing."

Stunned, I accepted the contract and made my way around the table saw and work tables, past the pegboard of hanging hammers and clamps and pliers and screwdrivers, out to Mrs. Lambert's office.

"He has no understanding of proper procedures," she said through immobile lips.

"Thank you," I stammered, and I walked out of the office into nearly three decades of job stability.

I'm not sure why, but my third period students not only sat in their chairs but they looked at me with expectation.

"Today we are going to study the art of first aid," said I. Nobody moaned. No spitballs flew. No farts sounded. So I continued. "I think we will all agree that crisis management skills are key to our survival, so not only will we learn how to revive somebody who is suffocating, but we will practice proper punctuation."

I had noticed the careful use of commas, colons, and periods in the first-aid book, and I remembered that in the last class I'd attended before abandoning my formal education, the teacher had been adamant that we understand the different usage of semicolons, colons, and end marks.

"Miss McFigg," said Peggy Smithson, chewing on her ponytail. "Can I ask a question?"

"Of course," I replied, preparing for the worst—a sarcastic remark, a double-entendre dig, some reference to my weight.

"Do you believe it is good crisis management skills to, say, borrow something that's not yours to avoid, say, being sent away and losing everything you love?"

Double-think, double-think, shrieked my mind, going into high gear. This had to be a trick. Something about my theft of the library's copy of *The Call of the Wild*? And if I answered wrong? *Be very careful, Zelda.* "Let me see if I understand," said I. "The question was, is borrowing good crisis management?" I would not fall for this ponytailed vixen's trap and lose my teacher's contract and extra forty dollars a week—enough to pay off the lien on Mrs. Mendelson's incinerated house and forge a new path to financial stability. "Class, what do you think about this question? Remember, crisis management involves a crisis."

The class looked blank but I waited. Finally Peggy raised her hand again. "Peggy?" I said expectantly, hoping she would answer the riddle and spare me a mess.

"Specifically," she said, drilling me with her turquoise eyes. "Specifically, if a person knew she would be sent away—far, far away—to, say, Sweden?"

Suddenly I remembered the swiped algebra exams, and I smiled. Peggy, recognizing my recognition, blushed. She was testing me. Seeing whether I would be her confidante. Now that I knew, I would let her worry. Drawing out my response just enough to keep the upper hand, I said, "So specifically, you want to know whether it's okay in a crisis—a matter of life or death, happiness or devastation, prom or no prom—whether it's ever okay to *borrow* something that is not necessarily up for loan? Is that the question?"

Peggy nodded, nervously twisting her ponytail around her index finger and glancing at the floor.

"Well, after careful thought, I would say that it is up to the borrower, and, in fact, it's nobody else's business."

A sneaky smile played on the sides of Peggy's perfectly painted lips. And so began our tacit understanding: I would not tattle on her, and she would give me the "cool" stamp of approval—an approval that none of her classmates understood, but that they would accept out of respect for her position as queen of the cool clique.

I am not a stupid woman. I knew I could not have twelve-, thirteen-, and one fourteen-year-old performing lip-to-lip resuscitation without causing an uproar that might result in another appearance of Sheriff Bodwell. So after the class read the introductory asphyxia text, I split them into groups of two to *mime*—as in Marcel Marceau if he were reviving an imaginary unconscious partner—I repeat, they were to *mime* this crisis-management action. My intention was to use the steps to focus their hyperactive brains.

"Tilt the head back and pull your partner's jaw up," I directed the adolescent anarchists. "Open your suffocating victim's mouth. Take a deep breath, open your mouth wide, and *pretend* to place it over—"

In hindsight I should have known what would happen. In hindsight, the outcome was predictable, considering that most of the children had self-selected into boy/girl pairs, and I'm extremely grateful that no word of the make-out debacle reached Principal Appleton's office or the over-sexed, rampantly procreating Moose Country parents. But there was one outcome that nobody could have foreseen.

When Donny Sherman kissed Peggy Smithson, something happened to both of them. I believe Donny *was* rescued from strangulation, because he began to breathe. With his whole body, he breathed—shedding layer after layer of fat during the subsequent months, exposing an arresting handsomeness. Peggy changed too. Her cold turquoise eyes turned soft aquamarine. And from that moment on, the two were inseparable.

Chapter 12

Lurleen Lagerfelt, the Moose Country guidance counselor and home ec. teacher, was, in my opinion, certifiably demented. Even though there was clearly nothing unstable about Donny Sherman, she announced—after the initial consultation, after the *Charlotte's Web* debacle—that she would see him for weekly appointments for the remainder of the term. I knew even then that the woman had ants in her pants and ill intent.

"What do you talk about?" I asked Donny during one of what had quickly become our customary after-school *tête-à-têtes*.

"I dunno," he answered with a slight smile. "This and that. That and this. You know how it is."

I didn't know how it was, but his smile was so endearing and admiring that I lost my train of thought. I was so pleased that he still liked visiting with me even though he'd begun slimming down and washing, instantly losing the bad body odor, and was now going with the most popular girl in the seventh grade. Although I'd discouraged it, by our second meeting, he'd even begun addressing me as Zelda, insisting that we were friends. What could I do? The boy had a mind of his own, and, in the land of middle school, time moved differently: In the space of a week, deep relationships formed and just as quickly dissolved. Boys and girls went steady, faculty alliances glued and unglued, and I felt as if Donny and I had known each other for a lifetime. "Zelda," he called me, giving me that look of gentle amusement and deep knowing. "Zelda, Zelda, Zelda," he almost chanted, wiping clean my board, "how did I ever survive without you?"

"How are things with Peggy?" I asked because his steady gaze was turning my brain to mush. "I hear she's doing quite well in algebra. Are you studying together?"

"I suppose you could call it that," said Donny, fiddling with my sponge. "Do you want me to wipe down anything else for you, Zelda?"

"If you like," I answered, beginning my own end-of-day tidying and relieved by our mutual physical activity. "The desk where Templeton sits is filthy. The boy never wipes his feet."

"Okey-dokey," said Donny, heading for the back row.

"Those shoes he wears look fit for a six-footer. He must be stuffing them with Kleenex. And they bring in the whole darned mud road. Speaking of which, did you remember to bring your bicycle pump? My tires need plumping."

"About that," said Donny, scrubbing Vermont clay off Templeton's chair legs. "How'd you like my grandfather's VW bug instead?"

"I don't know how to drive. Besides, I'm guessing your grandfather might have some thoughts about that."

"He doesn't use it," said Donny. "It just sits in the mud hole where he parked it ten years ago."

"I don't know how to drive."

"I could teach you," said Donny, stooped over the chair looking up at me sideways. "You could get a learner's permit if you're worried about being legal."

Because it was undignified, not to mention uncomfortable, for an approximately two-hundred-thirty-seven-pound lady to ride to work on a child's bicycle, I agreed to the driving lesson. Also, I wanted to meet Donny Sherman's grandfather and see where they lived. I knew from the other teachers that Grampa Sherman was unpredictable—that if he was sober, he could appear charming and reasonable and deeply concerned about his grandson's academic endeavors. But if he was on a bender, watch out. Considering my background with my mother, I assumed whatever state he was in, I could handle it. Nobody had seen the man for months, so I assumed the worst.

The following Friday, Donny plumped up my tires in preparation for my Sunday excursion. I'd agreed to ride my bicycle to Donny and his grandfather's house about a mile into the woods at the south end of town where you either hit the highway to Canada or disappeared into Native American-owned lands that nobody but Grampa Sherman and Donny cared to inhabit. The plumbing and electrical lines stopped short of the woods, and in these days before cell phones, there was no communication.

I tried to ride down the boulder-laden, bucketed dirt road to Donny's house, but my child-size bicycle seat was rough on my substantial adult bottom. So a few feet into the woods, I got off and walked the bike. I don't know which was more intimidating, the "No Trespassing" signs hand-painted in blood-drip red, or the canopy of brush and trees so dense that it blocked out the sun and sky and the road itself before and beyond my footstep. Within seconds, I lost all sense of direction and dealt with it by concentrating on my feet. Donny had warned me that if I got distracted by the bird sounds, I could end up in one of his grandfather's traps, so I ignored the hoots and caws and sudden rush of flapping wings and put one foot in front of the other, deeper and darker into the woods. I suppose I should have been frightened. After all, I had no idea where I was or where I was heading. But I trusted Donny's directions, and there was something hypnotic about the path with its mica rocks that glittered despite only the most occasional sliver of sunlight, and the trickling of unseen brooks, and no sign of human beings anywhere. Donny had said this was a protected habitat and, because all the young Indians had moved away or were working at casinos, Grampa Sherman, who was too drunk to travel, had gotten his tribal council to designate him the land's sole steward. He was given a monthly stipend and allowed to hunt and trap what he needed to eat and have his home at no cost. I suppose I should have been apprehensive about going off the main road into a dark forest to meet two men all by myself, but, to tell you the truth, it never occurred to me.

"Zelda!" called a voice I couldn't see. "You're almost here. The clearing is just a few more feet."

"I'm coming, Donny, I'm coming," I yelled into the impenetrable distance.

The VW bug was buried up to its back fender in mud on a downhill slope.

"Where's your grandfather?" I asked, looking up the hill at the shack, which had such a leftward tilt that it seemed poised for collapse. "I don't know anything about tires, but I think we're going to need some help to push this thing out of the mud."

"Don't worry, we can do it ourselves," said Donny with a twinkly smile. "I've got leverage." Then he gestured toward an iron contraption that looked like a giant straight-edged scissor with a winding handle. "My grampa invented this," he said proudly. "We just have to slide it under the back end."

For an hour, we heaved and shoved and hoisted and wound. Had I known what was involved, I never would have agreed to it. Several more times I asked about Grampa Sherman, and each time Donny answered that the man was busy and we could do the job without him.

Although I had to go to the bathroom, I decided to forego relief; I could see the outhouse up the hill, adjacent to the shack. It looked like an oversized telephone booth with the same leftward lean as the shack, and I was not about to suffer the humiliation of being rescued from a collapsed toilet. I was hot from our work, but, for the same reason, I declined Donny's offer of lemonade.

Around three o'clock, we finally got the leverage machine under the rear end of the car, and Donny directed me to sit in the driver's seat and start the engine. I was relieved to sit, and I crossed my legs as tight as a large lady can.

"Step on the clutch, shift the stick, and floor the gas," directed Donny.

"Oh my God," I yelled, as the car shot forward out of the hole up the hill heading straight for the shack.

"Take your foot off!" hollered Donny. "Brake it!"

"What?" I yelled as the outhouse loomed in front of me. And that's when I saw it. The birds. The bones. The body. Spread eagle on top of the outhouse roof was a skeletal body covered with feeding crows. At the sound of my shriek, they momentarily looked up, then resumed feeding on the corpse. In my horror, my feet went limp, and the car rolled backwards toward the mud hole.

"The brake! The brake!" yelled Donny, running toward me, gesticulating. "The peddle next to the gas!"

"What the hell is that?" I gasped, stamping on the brake an inch short of the hole. "Is that Grampa Sherman on the roof of the outhouse? Is he dead? What the hell's going on here, Donny?"

"Don't move," said Donny softly. And carefully he opened the driver's side door. "I'm just going to—" and he leaned his whole body over my lap and pulled up the hand brake. "Yup, that's Grampa. He died almost a month ago. Are you going to tell on me?"

"Why is he on top of the outhouse?"

"It's where he slept," said Donny. "Are you going to tell?"

I have almost no memories of my father. As I've said, he left before I was five. But I do remember he was a hunter. There wasn't much to hunt in suburban New York, but that didn't stop him from blowing away anything that wandered into our backyard—mostly bunnies, and once a doe. I remember her well: One minute she was standing there, minding her own business, munching tulips, and the next, she was down, still blinking as my father slit her throat. What was most shocking was how quickly she became meat.

A crow took flight with what looked like Grampa Sherman's shoelace dangling from its beak.

"Are you going to tell on me?" repeated Donny.

All my life, I'd lied, condemned, or run away when things were too hard—from home, to school, to New York City and my nonexistent theatrical career. Donny was a beautiful, albeit confused and desperate, boy who'd done a very bad thing—but not that much worse than what I'd done when I'd left my mother passed out in her studio. And now he needed my protection to survive. "No," I answered, "I will not tell. Now how about you teach me to drive?"

"Release the clutch," yelled Donny. We were on our second lap around the circular dirt track behind the shack, and Donny had his head in his hands like my mother with a migraine. "Let it up. You're stripping the gears," he begged.

I had no idea what he was talking about, but the rasping, rattling noise from the floor made me pull both feet off both pedals, and the car stalled. Silence. Donny chewed the inside of his mouth and looked out the passenger side window and I stared straight ahead. "Why did he sleep on the roof?" I finally asked.

Donny shrugged. "Something about the stars."

Donny had taught himself to drive when he was eight, but he was a very bad teacher. We decided it would be best if he kept the car. In a few weeks he would turn fifteen and get a learner's permit; then he could drive himself to school and I would act as his guardian for anything that required a signature. And Monday he would accompany me to buy a used car—an automatic with power steering advertised in the local penny saver for five hundred dollars, no returns.

We decided to leave Grampa Sherman on the outhouse roof until the birds were done, then Donny would bury the bones in the woods. We agreed that it would be best if I did not know the details.

Donny liked to strategize. I am more of a wing-it kind of girl.
But since I liked Donny and wanted to make him feel respected and
safe, I put up with the plotting and plans, agreeing to most everything. When we had concluded our conversation, we shook hands
like business partners, squeezed my bicycle into the back seat of the
VW, and Donny drove slowly to my house with me gesticulating
like a driving instructor in case we were observed.

Although he put up a confident front, I could tell by the way he
was driving that Donny was unnerved by the sudden exposure of
his grandfather. So when he confided that he would prefer not to
be alone for the rest of the night, I understood.

As I mentioned, I lived in a minuscule, one-room gate cabin, so
privacy was not an option. But I want to assure you that I main-
tained my professional teacher's boundary that night. We took
turns in the bathroom changing into our night attire—me in a
slightly smoke-damaged antique neck-to-floor nightie—salvaged
from the fire—that I'd borrowed from Matilda the drug addict's
grandmother at the same time that I'd picked up the muumuu;
Donny in his boxer shorts. I was happy to provide him with his
very first indoor shower, his first sense of safety, his first truthful
friendship, and I understood when he took a long time before coming to bed.

I told Donny I was a virgin. He said he was too, although from
the way he and Peggy Smithson looked at each other, I doubt it. We
agreed to sleep side-by-side with no hanky panky—except for one
ever so brief fondle of my left breast through my nightie. Donny
said it was beautiful. I thanked him. And miraculously, we both
fell into a deep sleep.

Just as one shoe size does not fit all feet, all of society's rules do not apply to all individuals' circumstances. Like me when I'd left my mother, Donny Sherman was mature beyond his years. He said he would eventually inform the Abenaki Tribal Council of his grampa's demise, but only after he'd proved that he had handled the job as forest steward for so long, doing it so well that they would not take his house away. How could I tattle and lose him his home? A home that he, in fact, had run for more than half of his young life. It was Donny who installed a generator so he and his grampa could refrigerate food. It was Donny who set and cleared the traps, skinned and cooked the catch, planted and harvested the vegetable garden, and enrolled himself in the Moose Country school system. Grampa Sherman was illiterate, Donny confided. He had never read Mr. London's *The Call of the Wild*. It was Donny who had read the story to his grampa. It was Donny who forged signatures on his report cards and dealt with the land inspectors when they came. It was Donny who wrote letters to the United States Patent and Trademark Office, eventually obtaining the rights to his grampa's car leverage contraption—which he sold at age twenty-eight to a large farm equipment company for enough money to finance his life as a bum. So do not judge me for keeping his secret and sleeping with him, *sans* sexual intercourse, twice in twenty-seven years. But I'm getting ahead of myself.

Monday morning, we drove most of the way to school in the VW bug, then just before the turn-off to the brick octopus driveway, I got out and rode my bike. Donny parked the bug in the faculty lot, and we entered the school separately, five minutes apart.

"Good morning, Miss McFigg," said Mrs. Lagerfelt, as we both headed for our classrooms. "Did you have a good weekend?"

Lurleen Lagerfelt was six feet tall with a mane of thick red curls that she flipped and tossed and twined around fingers that rivaled those of that diva of self-conscious manicures, Barbra Streisand (rumored—fueled by Lagerfelt's demure refusal to directly answer the question—to be her distant cousin, but I don't believe it).

"My weekend was superb," she chirped, despite the fact that I hadn't answered her question. "My husband took me to The Oasis for our anniversary." The Oasis was an overpriced weekend getaway patronized by rich city folk who migrated north during the summer. "I told him it was too much, but he insisted," said Lagerfelt looking down at my four-foot-eleven-inch frame with a coy smile. Then with the alertness of a hungry carnivore smelling blood, she demanded, "Tell me about *your* weekend."

"Quite nice," I answered with no hint that I'd slept with Donny Sherman.

"So how is Donny Sherman doing?"

The woman was a good, but I was better. "He's doing very well," I replied. "Your sessions must be helping him."

"Well, I certainly hope so," said Lagerfelt, boring into my eyes with her own, determined to pilfer my secret. "He speaks quite highly of you. I see such potential in the boy. College and maybe more. I'd love to expunge that entire unfortunate 'incident' from his record. I wonder how he's doing at home. You know he has a very difficult situation."

"Oh really?" I said with surprise. "No, I didn't know. Our relationship is strictly academic. He doesn't talk to me about his personal life. But he's doing quite well in my class. Very involved in assignments and a gifted original thinker."

Lagerfelt smiled with satisfaction and flipped her curls, assured that I had no secret and that her relationship with Donny was superiorly intimate to mine. "Well, do let me know if I can help— should he start having problems again."

"I certainly will," said I with a smile. The woman was a narcissistic slut.

Chapter 13

"When *The Story of Ferdinand* by Mr. Munro Leaf was published in 1936, it set off an enormous controversy," I said to my third period class. "Can anybody tell me why?"

Ignoring my lecture, Donny Sherman turned his moony eyes to Peggy Smithson. I knew it was just a performance to obscure our weekend's activity, and I admired his authenticity.

"I'll give you a hint: Ferdinand the bull lived in a place where it was expected that he would fight to the death, but instead he preferred to smell the flowers."

The class looked blank. Then the ersatz rat, Templeton, passed a note to the ersatz goose, Geraldine, and Peggy Smithson put her hand on Donny Sherman's leg under their desks.

"All right then. One more hint: The book was published nine months before the beginning of the Spanish Civil War. Spain is where they love to torture and kill bulls for sport."

More blank stares.

I decided to try a different tact. "Who here has not always done what everybody else does?"

Silence.

Giving up on my attempt to make another sweetgrass basket children's book relevant to libidinous seventh graders, I opened the book and read aloud: "Once upon a time in Spain there was a little bull and his name was Ferdinand..." And by the time I got to the picture of Ferdinand's shy little face looking out into the enormous bull fighting ring where the narcissistic Matador with the red cape and a sword as sharp as Lagerfelt's fingernails was so eager to kill him, I was near tears. "And *that*," I said with emphasis, "is why the really brave people break the rules! Please open your notebooks and write one hundred words about an experience when doing the sensible thing required going against the norm, and why Ferdinand the bull was heroic for preferring to smell the flowers."

The class looked perplexed. "Miss McFigg," said Donny.

"Yes, Donny," I answered, taking control of my facial muscles. "Are you all right?"

"Certainly," I answered. "I just think this is a very moving children's classic, and it would behoove us all to pay attention to its message."

The children wrote until the fourth period bell. Here is a sampling of their essays.

From Templeton:

> *What's the big deal about Ferdinand not fighting? So the bull was a coward. Who cares? And what's so hot about doing your own thing? Most of what most people do is stupid, so, yeah, I do whatever I want and I'm short, so nobody notices.*
> *The End.*

From Peggy Smithson:

> *I believe that Ferdinand the Bull was a true hero for staying true to himself and not getting killed just because other people thought he should. Breaking the rules is sometimes necessary, although I personally would never do it. Therefore I have chosen to be a law-abiding citizen and would only break the rules if it was a matter of life and death. I stay true to myself by being a law-abiding citizen, but I do have my own individual fashion style. I would never wear an unattractive outfit no matter how popular it was.*

From Donny Sherman:

> *Hi, Zelda. How are you doing? You seem a little upset about this Ferdinand book. Sorry about that. Okay, here's the assignment. Just tear off the top part of this and throw it away if you think that would be most discrete [sic].*
>
> *Why Ferdinand Is a Hero, and How I Am Like Him*
> *By Donny Sherman*
> *Being an Abenaki Indian in a town with very few left, I can relate very much to Ferdinand the Bull. I don't like fighting either, but when the bullying got to be too much, I*

felt like Ferdinand when he sat on the bum-
blebee who stung him and then I went wild
just like Ferdinand, so people thought I was
a crazy, mad Indian even though I wasn't.
Sometimes you just have to do what you've
got to to survive in this old world. And that's
how I went against the normal like Ferdi-
nand the Bull.

P.S. I don't regret it. After all, I got the girl!
P.P.S. Maybe tear off that last part if it
sounds un-discrete. See you later to buy the
car.

At lunchtime, I told Donny that I wasn't feeling well and would
have to take a rain check on the used car visit. I could feel Mrs.
Lagerfelt's eyes on me and, using my thespian training, I main-
tained a neutral demeanor for the entire conversation, which was
not easy. I had not had a bowel movement that morning due to my
general upset as well as pleasure at having an overnight guest. And
because I cannot poop in public restrooms, I was anxious to get
home posthaste.

Alas, this was not to be. Lagerfelt requested a faculty *tête-à-tête*
at the closing bell, and I was forced to gird my bursting loins for
yet another three-quarters of an hour.

"I'm just saying I think those of us who have given years of our
lives to this institution should be compensated more and have cer-

tain privileges beyond those of certain people who have only just started," said Lagerfelt to the annoyed group of teachers.

How she had deduced my salary was beyond me, and, like the crazed spear-carrying Banderilleros and Picadores and the narcissistic red-caped Matador in *Ferdinand*, she was determined to pick a fight. My salary was none of her business and I would not be dragged into a debate where I would be pushed to defend my nonexistent teaching experience. Furthermore, I suspected this entire confrontation had less to do with my salary than with Donny's inadvertent communication of his affection for me and Lagerfelt's obsession with the illusion of being Queen Bee in this provincial hive where all the males, with the exception of Donny, were married drones and prepubescent, pimply-faced, semi-literate boys with no prospects for the future.

"In my experience, salary information is a confidential matter," I said, politely addressing everybody and nobody. "I wasn't aware that there was a public record. If there is, I would be most eager to see it so that I might ascertain statistics for my use in future job negotiations with Principal Appleton."

An uncomfortable silence came over the group. Then Lagerfelt blushed and Mr. Chuck cleared his throat. "You have to understand," he said, looking directly at me, "we are a small town. I know things are different in the big city schools, but here—oh, hell, if Mrs. Lambert knows, we all know."

There was general shifting of bodies, then, smiling flirtatiously at Mr. Chuck and using the warm, throaty voice she used to speak to all men—including Donny Sherman—Lagerfelt intoned, "The point is we all do double-duty here, and it's unfair—"

"Will you can it, Lurleen!" said Mr. Chuck.

"Woody!" gasped Mrs. Gilhooley, the algebra and girls' gym teacher, and I began to laugh. Mr. Chuck's first name was Woody?

"Fuck you, Woody!" erupted Lagerfelt, bursting into tears like a spurned lover and completely forgetting her ingratiating voice. Then, swiping a dagger-size fingernail in my direction, "*She* thinks this is funny! Well, fuck her too!"

"I don't," I protested. "Honestly."

Mrs. Dorothy Gilhooley, a fifty-nine-year-old transplant from south Texas, pushed Lagerfelt back into her chair. "The truth is, Mrs. Lambert, bless her heart, is a disaster in the area of confidentiality—"

"As well as congeniality, joviality, and tonality—which is a drawback for a choir teacher," quipped Mr. Chuck, looking at Lagerfelt apologetically.

Lagerfelt blushed and forgave him. "As well as orality, psychosexuality, and several other categories of mentality dysfunction."

Mr. Chuck blew her a kiss, then Lagerfelt resumed her throaty voice: "I called this meeting because we have a union, and if one of us is able to negotiate the same salary for teaching one class that the rest of us earn doing double-duty—"

And that is how—in the interest of avoiding an unwinnable bloody battle and returning to my metaphorical cork tree to smell the flowers—I volunteered to teach dramatic arts . . . and therefore ended up directing yearly productions of twelve-, thirteen-, and fourteen-year-olds in *A Streetcar Named Desire* and *Long Day's Journey into Night*.

As with my English curriculum, I made up what I did not know, embodying my belief that invention is the most valuable life skill one can have or teach.

Chapter 14

"Pace yourselves!" hollered Dorothy Gilhooley. "You've got two more laps. Think!" And to punctuate the importance of the direction, she blew her gym coach's whistle and stamped her massive tennis shoe.

The girls' track team, led by Peggy Smithson, rounded the north loop of the dirt course adjacent to the parking lot. I was heading for my bike, full of thoughts about my new dramatic arts program. It was a week after our impromptu faculty meeting and I still didn't have a plan. But the sight of seven beautiful long-legged girls running like one perfectly balanced organism with seven ponytails swinging like synchronized windshield wipers stopped my mind and gave me an idea: I would do a musical, or a play with music and dance, for my first production.

Peggy's intense turquoise eyes saw nothing as she flew toward me. She was precision embodied: relaxed arms and wrists, long sleek legs moving powerfully, effortlessly in graceful, giant strides. Clearly the leader, she set the pace and the pulse for the girls at her flanks. They followed her unspoken directions, turning when she turned, arms and legs matching her rhythm and swing.

I didn't know anything about meditation, but I imagined it was something like these lean thoroughbred bodies in majestic, metronome motion. What would it be like to be graceful and powerful, I wondered. And that's when I saw Donny. He was sitting in the bleachers near the finish line, looking as mesmerized as I felt, and in love. Peggy, oblivious to anything but her stride, rounded in front of him, leading the pack into the next lap.

There was a truck parked beside the bleachers. It looked like Dorothy's husband. He was sitting in the driver's seat with binoculars, following the girls around the track.

"Pick up the pace!" hollered Dorothy, her awkward, angular body in sharp contrast to the girls' as she lurched from one side of the track's inner circle to the other to follow their progress.

Lord, how I wished I were thin.

As the girls rounded the north corner again, past me, past the east brick tentacle which housed my classroom, Dorothy's math room, and Lurleen Lagerfelt's home ec. room, I saw someone part the lowered Venetian blinds to watch. It was Lagerfelt. Who was she watching? It wasn't the girls. She was staring toward the bleachers, her eyes darting between Donny watching Peggy and Mr. Gilhooley with his binoculars.

As the girls went into the final lap, Mr. Gilhooley put down his binoculars and revved his engine. Lagerfelt let the blinds snap shut and, a few seconds later, she emerged from the main entrance to the school. She looked at Gilhooley's truck, then Donny in the bleachers, then strode past me to her car. Was I invisible?

"Let loose! Cut loose!" hollered Dorothy Gilhooley as the girls neared the north end, and Peggy kicked out her gazelle legs and broke away from the pack. Lord, was she beautiful!

Mr. Gilhooley revved his engine hard, Lagerfelt slammed her car door, and Donny leaned forward, grabbing his knees, his mouth gaping. "Go, Peggy, go!" he hollered. And Peggy, in a world of her own, arms and legs slicing air like fast-motion scissors, crossed the finish line. Gasping, she threw back her head, and her ponytail band broke, releasing a mane of blonde hair that shone like spun gold in the late afternoon sun.

Lagerfelt peeled out of the faculty lot, spraying gravel. Donny threw his arms to the heavens, then held his face and rocked. Mr. Gilhooley pulled out of his spot beside the bleachers, beeped twice and waved to this wife, then drove away. And Peggy loped slowly, catching her breath, oblivious to it all.

Dorothy Gilhooley blew her whistle as the last girl finished the course, and I shook the awe out of my head and continued across the parking lot to my bicycle. I would do a play with music and dance for our Christmas production; I would create a peaceful, happy, graceful life of financial stability whilst smelling the flowers; and I would lose thirty pounds by Thanksgiving or die trying.

Chapter 15

"Shuf-full-ball-change, shuf-full-ball-change, shuf-full, shuf-full, shuf-full, shuf-full."

The Christmas play was a disaster. I'd used up everything I knew from the two Taps Is Tops lessons I'd taken back in New York City, we'd filled only thirty seconds of the fifteen-minute musical interlude composed by Mrs. Lambert, and I was so light-headed from fasting that I thought I might faint. Our Christmas play—my own adaptation, *avec* song and dance, of the classic Grimm's fairytale, *The Frog Prince: A Metaphorical Play with Music*—starred Donny Sherman, and I'd been aiming for a heart-rending work of staggering genius.

"Miss McFigg, I still don't get it," said Jimmy Bodwell, the sheriff's son. He was part of the Greek chorus of tadpoles and would perform the tap routine signifying the impending danger to the king's beautiful daughter, played by Peggy Smithson. The shuffulls, along with flailing finger movements *à la* Diva Lagerfelt (an inside joke), signified the princess losing her golden ball (signifying her innocence), down the cool, deep well (signifying the home of the Frog Prince who, in exchange for retrieving the ball, would

demand that she play fair and love him the most as she'd promised).
"I don't get this shuf-full thing," said Jimmy Bodwell. "Can you
explain it again?"

"Let's take a break," I said to all the tadpoles. "We'll resume in
ten minutes."

I needed the break. For some reason, the concept of toe-tap-
ping, as opposed to full-foot dragging, eluded the prepubescent
amphibians, and their shuf-fulls were making my eyeballs explode.
I grabbed my purse and retreated to the teachers' restroom to break
my daylong fast with a soothing snack of cheese and peanut butter
sandwich crackers—my comfort food of choice since my days with
Mike the poet.

Every day I committed to a new fast, and every day, by late afternoon or early evening, I broke it with a binge, promising tomorrow
I would be better. Tomorrow I would definitely stop eating carbohydrates. I had read that they were addictive. I'd read that part of
dieting was learning to eat slower, so in preparation for tomorrow's
life change, I chewed each bite of cheese and peanut butter sandwich cracker ten times before swallowing. I liked eating this way.
It prolonged the pleasure. Yes, tomorrow I would remember that I
liked it as I ate nothing but carrots and broccoli. I would like myself
much better one hundred pounds lighter. I would like it if Donny
looked at me the way he had looked at—No, no, unacceptable
thought. Think of something else... Other things that I liked...

I liked the teachers' restroom. In fact, to my surprise, I liked the
entire brick octopus. I liked knowing where I would go every day,
what I would do. I was comfortable and felt validated by my position in spite of the fact that my entire academic background was
an invention. By November, I'd invented a curriculum of children's
books along with a smattering of state-required classical literature,
which I read for the first time along with my students. I'd written

a plausible seventh and eighth grade Language Arts Curriculum, complete with a grammar section straight out of the SAT English review book, plus an explanation of the metaphorical, philosophical, and metaphysical values, thinking, and writing skills that could best be developed and honed from exercising adult interpretation of children's literature. Appleton said mine was the most progressive English curriculum he'd ever seen and I was given free rein to invent my dramatic arts program.

By November, Donny Sherman, who had been driving freely for over a month without incident, taking Peggy Smithson on dates, had dropped all excess weight. The combination of growing five inches in three months, chopping and hauling wood at home, plus his new-found interest in working out in front of Peggy had indeed turned this frog into a prince, and all female eyes followed him as he strolled the Moose Country halls hand-in-hand with his girl.

Lurleen Lagerfelt ended her affair with Mr. Chuck and moved on to Harry the janitor. When that got old, she returned her attention to Donny—scheduling his counseling appointments for three o'clock on Fridays. I was sure the woman was a nymphomaniac, but when I asked Donny about his sessions, he just smiled and answered, "Oh you know, this and that, that and this." Had he been less mature, I'd have worried about him and perhaps notified Moose Country Social Services. But he assured me that I was the only one he had confided in, and all was well in all personal departments.

I felt a little lonely Friday afternoons, and perhaps it showed because shortly before the Thanksgiving break, Dorothy Gilhooley, who had seventeen rescued cats and six mongrel dogs and said there was always room for one more, invited me to her celebratory feast. Because Donny was eating with the Smithsons and would not require my surrogate parenting, I accepted the invitation.

Our *Frog Prince* rehearsal was the last we'd have before the Thanksgiving vacation, and I was concerned that it was cataclysmic. I'd been in the bathroom at least ten minutes—enough time for Jimmy and the other tadpoles to turn into frogs. Break time was up and I supposed I should return to the auditorium but the thought filled me with panic and sorrow. So instead I opened my last package of cheese and peanut butter sandwich crackers and pondered what Ed Sullivan would do if faced with such amateurism. And that's when I had my epiphany: I would adapt Mike the poet's song/ poem, "Dusty Rose," as an oral recitation to the accompaniment of Mrs. Lambert's musical interlude, thus filling the hole in the play and alleviating myself and the tadpoles of public humiliation. The idea was so efficient and ingenious that I nearly choked on my snack crackers in my hurry to swallow before racing back to rehearsal.

"Hello!" I bellowed over the jackhammer taps. "Hello! May I have your attention please! Tadpoles, royal family, and frogs!" (I had several back-up frogs in case Donny lost his voice or backed out or was too busy with Peggy and Lagerfelt to learn his part properly.) "May I have your attention please!"

Gradually the students quieted. I had learned that if I waited long enough after yelling, they would eventually look at me to see why I was no longer yelling.

"I have an announcement," I continued. "We are going to drop the tadpole tap dance and substitute a recitation of a distinguished poem that was famously performed on the *Ed Sullivan Show*—"

"Who?" said a frog.

"Never mind. It is a great work of literature that we will recite *en masse*. Your parents will recognize it. I will pass out the words after Thanksgiving. Class dismissed." And I was nearly trampled in the exodus by all but Donny—who smiled brilliantly and saluted. The boy was a such a joy.

Considering my history, it may come as a surprise to hear that my least favorite thing, besides mice, is negotiating unknown situations. I had intended to spend the days before Thanksgiving fasting and integrating "Dusty Rose" into *The Frog Prince*, but I was too apprehensive to write and too needy of comfort to fast. Dinner with the Gilhooleys was a possible landmine. For two days, all I could think about was making a wrong move that would reveal one or all of my inventions, resulting in my instant ruination due to the fact that Dorothy Gilhooley, bless her heart, was a habitual blabberer with no brain-to-mouth filter.

"So where are your people from, Zelda?" asked Ralph Gilhooley as his wife ladled a mountain of sweet potatoes onto his already overloaded plate and shooed dogs and cats away from the dinner table.

I thought for a long time, pretending to admire the panting and mewing menagerie, hoping to appear too distracted to remember such a mundane fact about my life. "Oh, here and there, there and here," I quipped, smiling ingratiatingly. "This is some water. Is it imported?"

Ralph Gilhooley looked alarmed. "Something wrong with it?" He was a retired Green Mountain Railroad conductor and he took travel very seriously.

"I just meant it's good. Is it one of those bottled waters from Europe?"

"Vermont tap water," said Dorothy placatingly. "Shoo, Morton. Your food's in the kitchen."

"Mmm good," I said, drinking deeply and looking at the huge hound as he flopped to the floor and laid his head on Dorothy's enormous foot.

"Zelda worked in New York City schools before she came here," said Dorothy. "So tell us—"

"Earthshoe!" I shouted. "That's where my people come from. Earthshoe, New York, a little town—just a tiny village really; nobody's heard of it—about an hour north of the Hudson River. It's where they make Earth Shoes—which I see you like, Dorothy. What a coincidence!"

"You don't say," said Dorothy. "Are your parents still—"

"My father, bless his heart, was a wonderful man. Worked in the plant till he died. We all loved the shoes. My mother especially, since she was on her feet so much. She was a baker. McFigg's Bakery and Cooked Goods Shoppe. Everybody bought bread and baked casseroles from my mother. She died on her feet. Got stuck in one of the walk-in ovens. It was a tragedy. Everybody in Earthshoe mourned her passing and the subsequent lack of cherry tarts. Can I have some more turkey please? This is just a fantastic meal. White meat, if you don't mind."

Ralph gave Dorothy a funny look, and Dorothy ignored it and cut into the turkey. "You're a good eater, Zelda," said Ralph through a mouthful of sweet potatoes.

Had I not been so nervous, I might have taken offense at such a crass remark about my weight, but I was glad he was changing the subject. I was just about to forgive him when he winked at me with a secret sideways look at Dorothy, who was built like a large, lanky boy.

"Ralph likes a woman who enjoys her food," said Dorothy, missing her husband's expression as she slashed at the turkey. "Is this enough, dear?" she said placing at least six ounces of white meat on my plate. And she said it so sweetly that I suddenly felt like crying. "Mmm, good, thanks so much," I answered, swallowing hard. I had not cried since... to tell you the truth, I can't remember.

"Zelda is a wonderful teacher," prattled Dorothy. "I can't tell you what a difference she's made to some of the more difficult students. Donny Sherman, bless his heart, was just a lost little Indian before Zelda took him under her wing. How is he doing, Zelda? That grandfather is a disgusting drunkard. I always say a boy needs a mother. I don't suppose they're celebrating tonight. Not really an Indian holiday, I suppose, considering what followed. Shoo, Morton. Baby, stop bothering Topsy. Morton, no! I told you, no begging on Thanksgiving."

There was an awful lot of food here, and I suddenly wished I'd brought a secret plastic bag to secretly shove some of it into to take home for a snack. But it turned out there was no need.

Later that evening, Dorothy insisted on giving me enough turkey, stuffing, sweet potatoes, and pumpkin pie to feed me for an evening. "My goodness," I gasped, accepting the ten-pound bag, "I don't know what to say. This is enough for a month!"

Dorothy smiled and said, "Just keep the Tupperware, dear." And, although I was grateful, I could almost hear her remarking to the faculty: "Zelda, bless her heart, you should have seen her at Thanksgiving. She eats like a Wooly Mammoth."

Ralph offered to drive me home, and I congenially accepted. Night had fallen and I appreciated not having to walk two miles in the dark.

"So, did you enjoy the meal, Zelda?" he said as he started the engine. "Get enough to eat there?"

"Yes, thank you," I answered, quashing an impulse to tell him that he was carrying a few extra pounds himself, and I didn't appreciate comments about my body—particularly since both he and Dorothy had been relentless, urging me to eat more than my stomach could hold in one sitting. "It was a lovely meal, and I really appreciate you and Dorothy inviting me."

"You know Dorothy's barren," he said, apropos of nothing.

"Oh?" I answered, because it was the only thing that came to mind.

Ralph turned the wheel sharply and sprayed gravel as we sped out of his driveway and onto the road. "That's why she takes in all the strays. It's pathetic. So how about you? You got a boyfriend? You look like you could pop out some babies."

I glanced at the speedometer, calculating how many minutes this ride would take. "I'm not ready for all that yet," I replied politely.

"Career girl. Playing the field, are ya? It's good you're not married. Although that never stopped Lurleen Lagerfelt. Yeah, Lurleen and me, we had some fun." He smiled at me lasciviously and beeped his horn. "Don't say nothin' to the missus though. I wouldn't wanna hurt her. You career girls understand about all that, I expect."

"New York has a lot more street lights," I replied, peering into the darkness and suddenly understanding Lagerfelt's behavior at track practice. But Ralph Gilhooley? The woman had no taste.

As we came to the end of the two miles, he slowed the car, finally stopping in front of my gate cabin.

"Thanks for the meal and the ride and everything," I said, struggling with my seatbelt.

"Let me help you with that," said Ralph. And before I could protest, he was leaning over my stomach and shoving his bicep into my breasts.

All of the male species were pond scum, I decided later that evening as I consumed the entire bag of turkey, stuffing, sweet potatoes, and pumpkin pie. Every single one of them . . . except Donny Sherman. Tomorrow I would start a salad and tuna diet and be fifty pounds lighter by Christmas.

Chapter 16

I have always believed that I could be a great conductor except for the fact that I know nothing about music. I wanted to speed up Mrs. Lambert's insipid musical interlude so that it would end at the same time as the tadpoles' choral recitation of "Dusty Rose," but the woman wouldn't let me set the tempo. As a result, there were four and one-half minutes of atonal droning after my tadpoles had ceased speaking. It wasn't until our last rehearsal that I decided to insert a brief ballet to fill the void. It was a lot quieter than tap and was easily lifted from my sweetgrass basket three-book series, the *First, Second,* and *Third Steps in Ballet* by Ms. Thalia Mara, director of one of the major ballet schools in New York City.

"Does everyone remember their *assemblés avec port de bras?*" I queried.

"Bras!" shouted the tadpoles, pretending to have breasts.

"And even if you can't remember the steps," I continued, ignoring their puffed-out chests and mimes of breast fondling, "even if ballet totally eludes you, remember one thing: posture and placement! I'll say it once more—"

"Tits!" laughed the tadpoles.

Speaking was a waste of energy. So I prayed: "Please, God if you exist, help them to stand as straight as their tadpole costumes will allow, so that the audience and Principal Appleton don't notice that this is a train wreck."

It was a few minutes to performance. We were backstage in the Moose Country auditorium, and the escalating laughter and general commotion on the other side of the curtain had me in a cold sweat *avec* palpitations. "Where are my back-up frogs?" I frantically stage-whispered. I could see Donny. He had been dressed for an hour and a half and was fully prepared to perform, but my anxiety demanded a focus. "Frogs!" I nearly shouted. "Let me see you right this minute!"

"Right here, Miss McFigg," called Dickie Grayson, whose sweetness almost made up for his lack of coordination and singing ability. When I'd put out the call for understudies, he had been kind enough to volunteer himself along with two other members of the Moose Country Junior Debate Team. "Do you need us to step in?" he said hopefully.

"No, sweetheart. You look wonderful as extra tadpoles. Please join the ones pretending to have breasts. But should anything happen during the performance—"

"We know!" said the back-up frogs in unison. "We hop in!"

"Fine. Thank you. You look wonderful. Where's my clipboard? Oh, I'm holding it. Silly me." Then I pretended to blow my nose in order to channel my nervous energy and camouflage my distress. No point in transmitting it to the amphibians.

"Five minutes," said Mrs. Lambert, who was acting as stage manager as well as musical director. "Where is my percussion?"

A cacophony of tambourines and bongo drums answered, and Mrs. Lambert punched air, hissing, "Shush!"

"Are you ready, Donny?" I asked for the millionth time.

Donny smiled and nodded, his green painted arm locked around Peggy Smithson's princess-size waist. She did look lovely with her normally ponytailed blonde hair permed and highlighted and flowing down the back of her golden sequined antique gown. She had borrowed the dress from a costume museum in another county, and it looked as if it was made for her. "I did some teeny weenie alterations," she had confided when I'd asked about it during dress rehearsal.

"Places," hissed Mrs. Lambert, and Templeton, who I'd cast as the narrator because of his big voice, stepped center stage behind the crack in the curtains. Mrs. Lambert gave a downbeat to her orchestra, "And one, and two, and—," the violins screeched an atonal double-stop, signifying a fairytale with a dark and mysterious adult Christmastime subtext. The audience hushed, and Templeton stepped through the curtains.

"Once upon a time there was a beautiful young princess," he announced, and the curtains opened on Peggy Smithson preening in front of a cardboard mirror and winking at the audience.

Big laugh. Thank God. I crossed my arms in front of my clipboard and prayed some more.

"It was the day before Christmas," (my teeny weenie alteration to make the story holiday appropriate) "and the beautiful princess was bored with being so beautiful, so to amuse herself, she put on her worst bonnet and clogs—,"

Peggy Smithson, who had fought me every step of the way, reluctantly donned wooden shoes and a fishing hat from my sweetgrass basket, managing to shoot me a dirty look as she turned upstage. Then cocking the hat rakishly and turning up the brim to look cute, she rotated back to the audience, decimating my subtext of loneliness, alienation, and isolation due to the pressures of being perfect—especially at Christmastime with a dysfunctional family with no mother and a father who was a king.

"The lonely princess went for walk by herself," said Templeton, as if it were a struggle to stay awake. "She walked and walked and walked until she came to a cool spring of water. Cool because it was a hot spring that never froze, even the day before Christmas." (Again, a seasonal alteration—which also happened to work well as a metaphor for the ever-moving subconscious signified by the water.)

"Oh, what a beautiful pool of water," gushed Peggy. "I think I'll sit a spell." And she sank to the floor allowing her gown to balloon out in a perfect circle, framing her perfect figure as she gazed into the raised mirror, signifying the pool, admiring herself. Apparently the girl was oblivious to the basic dramatic conflict of appearance versus subtextual angst, awkwardness, rage, and insecurity that afflicted every adolescent girl besides her! "I think I'll play with my ball now," she sighed, shining a gleaming smile at the audience and admiring her reflection in the pool. "Oh where, oh where could my ball be?"

"Holy shit!" hissed Mrs. Lambert, realizing she'd forgotten to place the prop. And she hurled it on onstage, hitting Peggy square in the crotch.

"The princess loved her ball," said Templeton, sneering sideways at Peggy. "Almost as much as she loved herself." And although I hadn't written that line, I can't say that it upset me.

"Her ball was her favorite plaything; and she was always tossing it up into the air, and catching it again as it fell. And suddenly she threw it up so high that she lost track, and it fell down and down and down, disappearing into the spring," said Templeton.

Although we had rehearsed this sleight of hand at least a hundred times, Peggy managed to miss the bucket upstage of the mirror where the ball was suppose to disappear, signifying the loss of her soul—leaving her empty, hapless, hopeless, and helpless. Unruffled, she simply grabbed the ball and plunked it into the bucket, making

a loud hollow noise, because Mrs. Lambert had forgotten to insert
the foam-rubber lining. Thank goodness, the audience laughed.
Peggy did too, then resumed her character.

"Oh, no," she squeaked in a little girl voice, "my ball has fallen
way down deep into the spring. Alas! If I could get my ball again,
I would give all my fine clothes and jewels, and everything that I
have in the world."

And right on cue, Donny, bless his heart, popped his head out
of another upstage hiding place and, in a British accent—his own
invention; I take no credit—he said, "Why, hallo there, most beautiful lady!" and the audience roared.

To say I was proud is understatement. I was so relieved and torn
up with emotions that I missed the next few minutes as Donny got
Peggy to promise that she would love him best and let him live with
her if he retrieved her precious gold ball soul. And even though the
spoiled princess never intended to keep the bargain, she agreed.

"Then the frog dove deep under the water," said Templeton,
suppressing a yawn. "And after a while he came up with the ball
in his mouth."

"My ball, my ball," shrieked Peggy in that way of oversexed girls.
And she grabbed it and ran offstage.

"Wait, you promised!" cried Donny so forlornly it was all I could
do not to run onstage to rescue him. "Please take me!"

Suppressing a cry, I hugged my clipboard, and nodded to Mrs.
Lambert.

"And a-one, and a-two," she hissed, waving her arms at the recal-
citrant orchestra, and so began the fifteen-minute atonal musical
interlude.

"Enter tadpoles!" I stage-whispered at the five of them, who
apparently had forgotten all about the play and were involved in a
game of craps. "'Dusty Rose' tadpoles—*Now!*"

"Oh, jeez," gasped Dickie, rallying the others onto the stage. "I am *so* sorry."

And they began.

You may recall that "Dusty Rose" is the story a girl with buttocks-length auburn hair who longed to be a ballerina but didn't have the body because she was too Rubinesque, so in disappointment she kills herself. Well, I made a teeny weenie alteration whereby I transposed the Rubinesque girl into the frog, who longed to be a prince so that the princess would love him as she'd promised—illustrated by the tadpole ballet—and at the end, instead of killing himself, he dives into the upstage hiding place, signifying deep into the water of his unconscious.

The tadpoles completed their ballet without killing each other, and since they were still out of sync with the musical interlude, they simply waited for it to end.

Silence. Not a sound in the auditorium.

Yes! I thought. *Yes!* Finally an audience had seen and felt the depth of my soul through my artistic expression. And in a state of bliss at the validation of my life's passion, I began to applaud.

"Good God!" exclaimed somebody in the audience, and then all hell broke loose. There was so much hooting and shouting and jeering and laughing that Donny almost missed his cue to explode out of the hole and race to claim his princess. Templeton, bless his heart, did his best to overpower the crowd with his booming narration, but it was hopeless.

Unfortunately, I was not the only one in shock at the audience's reaction. We had held the "Dusty Rose" segment rehearsal privately in the last few minutes of the dress rehearsal and nobody but me had seen it. At the sound of the jeers, the cast looked as if they had been struck by lightning. And then gradually they, too, began to giggle.

Finally, Donny, the only real trooper in the company, pulled himself together. Shouting over the roar of the audience, he insisted that the princess open her heart to him, and despite the fact that the King forgot his lines demanding that his daughter keep her promise, Donny did the slow turn we'd practiced, transforming into the prince he'd been before he'd been cursed by a spiteful fairy.

"He gazed at the princess with the most beautiful eyes she had ever seen," shouted Templeton over the audience, "and standing at the head of her bed, he addressed her thusly:"

"*You*," said Donny to Peggy, not caring if he could be heard. "*You* have broken this cruel charm, and now I have nothing to wish for but that you should go with me into my father's kingdom, where I will marry you, and love you as long as you live."

Then as Donny kissed Peggy, the curtain closed to thunderous boos and fart sounds.

I wanted to die.

I had just finished two pints of Rocky Road ice cream when the phone rang later that evening. "Hello?" I answered.

"Hey," said Donny.

"Donny?" He didn't have a telephone, so I instantly knew where he was.

"Yeah," said Donny. "Are you okay, Zelda? You ran out pretty fast after the show."

"Where's Peggy?"

"Fighting with her mom. I got plenty of time. So are you okay? Listen, I know you're not. I just wanted to tell you, it doesn't matter, Zelda. You got to let it roll over you. 'Like the wind,' my grampa used to tell me. Basically we're all lying on top of outhouses, and when the stink comes, you got to let it blow by."

"Right."

"So I just wanted to say that. I love you, Zelda. It's gonna be okay. Trust me." And he hung up.

Chapter 17

Donny Sherman was right. Everything was okay. Much to my amazement, Principal Appleton was so pleased with my work that he gave me a raise and asked if I would start a school newspaper. It seems the head of the PTA had been in the audience; she was a slightly deaf former actress whose claim to fame was understudying one of Tevya's daughters in a summer stock road company of *Fiddler on the Roof.* Although she'd left early—before the blessed musical interlude—she'd told Principal Appleton that the production was "revolutionary." She said whoever had conceived it should be applauded for her out-of-the-box creativity. Not only that, but it turned out, despite the boos and fart sounds, the play was loved by the couple of newer Moose Country parents who had recently moved north, transplanting their children into this godforsaken woods to live a more natural lifestyle and transform from big-city nonachievers into high-performing illiterates due to the dearth of academic competition. They wrote to Appleton that being at my play was the funniest, campiest, most entertaining evening they'd had in Moose Country and they thanked him for his forward-thinking leadership to let middle schoolers do such experimental work.

I accepted my raise and posted a notice on the cafeteria bulletin board for student reporters and editors for the new *Middle School Mutterer*. Then I bought a television set and a used car. I wanted to be a normal, happy Moose Country, Vermont, US of A, citizen, to go to the movies, to have friends, and to invite them over to watch the Academy Awards while eating snacks and making snide remarks. It was 1983, I was twenty-two years old, and I told Donny Sherman that I was ready to learn to drive.

"Brake it!" barked Donny. "Jeez, Zelda, I thought you said you were gonna buy an automatic."

It was five o'clock on Thursday and we were practicing U-turns in the faculty parking lot. Nobody was around. No parked cars to hit. But still I panicked and stalled every time I changed directions. We were in my new 1972 VW bug, just like Grampa Sherman's, which I bought because it cost one hundred dollars and the seller swore he'd only driven it to and from the market.

"Okay, let's try again," said Donny in a patronizing tone that he believed was soothing. "Turn the ignition, step *gently* on the gas, and wait for it to catch. Are you in neutral?"

"Yes, I'm in neutral," I snapped.

"Are you sure?" said Donny. His tone reminded me of how I imagined my father sounded talking to my mother when she was blind drunk and he was secretly planning his get-away.

"Yes, I'm sure. And would you mind not talking to me like I'm an imbecile? I'm six and one-half years older than you." Donny just stared at the stick shift. "Oh, sorry," I said, seeing that it was in first.

"The clutch, the clutch," stage-whispered Donny, suppressing his tone.

"That's much better," I said, stepping on the clutch and smoothly down-shifting to neutral. "Okay, ignition…"

"Engine!" announced Donny as the car came to life.

"And…blast off!" said I, stepping gently on the gas with my right foot, the clutch with my left, shifting effortlessly to first gear, and slowly releasing the clutch. Upon executing a perfect U-turn to the north end of the brick octopus, I stopped without stalling.

"Excellent," said Donny.

"I know," said I. "I have an excellent teacher. Good thing I studied tap dancing. I never realized driving required so much choreography." And we both sighed.

"Zelda," said Donny.

"Yes," I answered.

"Do you think we could go to the movies sometime?"

I felt a knot in my throat the size of a baby's fist. Since I could not speak, I shifted to neutral, ever so carefully pressing and releasing the clutch. Then I pulled the handbrake to stop, and put my hand on Donny's arm, above his elbow, sliding up to the bicep that he'd been working so hard to enlarge. Donny didn't move, so I left my hand there, feeling the bulge under his shirt. Swallow as I might, the baby's fist would not go down. I moved my hand up to Donny's neck and massaged the back of it—the soft spot just under his long black hair.

"Oh," sighed Donny, and that's when we saw her.

We'd thought we were alone because it was five o'clock. There were no cars, but you could always count on Lurleen Lagerfelt to pop up unexpectedly. That day, of all days, her husband had driven her to work, and as she stepped out of the school to wait for him to pick her up, she saw us. And seeing our shock at her seeing us was all the confirmation she needed that something tawdry was going on. Something so awful that it merited a vitriolic report, hand-delivered to Principal Appleton the next morning.

"Let me take care of this," said Donny.

"Okay," said I. "Okay."

First thing the next morning, Donny was called to Principal Appleton's office. I hadn't slept and it was all I could do to supervise homeroom and study hall, let alone teach a class on journal writing basics plus the emotional ramifications of living a hidden life based on *The Diary of Anne Frank*. Any minute I expected to be summoned, terminated, and possibly led away in handcuffs. I could just see Sheriff Bodwell's self-satisfied expression as he pushed me into his squad car. "Miss McFigg is a deviant," he'd announce on his red megaphone. "I always knew it."

I was just finishing lunch—a bowl of alphabet soup and twelve individually wrapped packets of Saltine crackers was all I could get into my nervous stomach—when I happened to glance out the window to the main entrance. Oh, how I wish I'd learned lip reading instead of finger spelling when my fifth grade class had divided into study groups following a reading of *The Story of Helen Keller* by Ms. Lorena A. Hickok, a lovely writer—which, come to think of it, might follow nicely after Anne Frank: two stories of women who lived in the dark; I have a weakness for consistent themes. But as I was saying, lip reading would have been an asset, because all I could see was Lurleen Lagerfelt's spastic mouth as she went ballistic. She began swatting at Appleton who was hanging onto her arm. Then her husband peeled up in his car, jumped out, and bullied her into the passenger's seat. There followed a heated conversation *avec* much gesticulation between Messrs. Lagerfelt and Appleton, while Lurleen, now chastened, stared stoically out the windshield.

Finally the two men shrugged, shook hands, and Mr. Lagerfelt got into the driver's seat and drove away.

That was the last the student body saw of Lurleen Lagerfelt until graduation—which she attended thirty pounds lighter with a drugged look of pleasantness on her over-made-up face. But I'm getting ahead of myself.

"What on earth happened?" I demanded of Donny later that day. "What on earth did you say to Appleton?"

The closing bell had rung an hour ago, and Donny and I had waited an additional hour—me, puttering around my classroom; Donny doing I don't know what—before convening in the parking lot. We checked classroom windows. Nobody. Appleton had cut out early, as was his habit on Fridays. And there were no cars in the lot.

"What the hell happened, Donny?" I demanded again.

Donny smiled cryptically. "A little of this, a little of that," was all he would say.

We did my driving lesson, made a date to see a movie that weekend, then drove home to our respective houses in our respective automobiles despite the fact that neither of us possessed a driver's license.

Chapter 18

Sunday afternoon, just as we'd planned, Donny drove to my house. Then, taking back roads, we both drove in my car to the Moose Country mall to see the first showing of the 1979 award-winning movie *Being There* starring Mr. Peter Sellers. The movie was billed as the hilarious story of a simple, illiterate gardener who ends up being an advisor to the President of the United States because of misunderstandings about his name and background.

In New York, this would have been called a revival house, but in Moose Country they were just regular movies that happened to be old by the time they made their way this far north—they were old movies that nobody but a few old people wanted to see, so there was almost nobody in the theatre and we had our choice of seats. Donny chose two in the center, the second row from the back. And wouldn't you know it, just as the coming attractions were finishing, a couple hurried down the aisle, sliding in two rows in front of us in the same two seats.

"Do you want to switch?" I whispered. Donny had warned me beforehand that he didn't like talking while anything was playing— even coming attractions. He shook his head and motioned for me to hush. And as the MGM lion growled, he leaned back in his seat like he was in his backyard surveying his property, and he smiled.

The first scene was a stark black and white farmhouse. A truck rolled in and then, in big red letters came the title of the movie: HAIR.

"Hey," I said.

"Don't worry about it," whispered Donny. "I heard this one's good too." The boy was imperturbable.

Okay, I thought. *Okay.*

What followed was a story about a man named Berger who reminded me a little of Mike the poet, except that he was less drugged and nicer. He ends up taking the place of the guy from the black and white farmhouse. The farm guy is named Claude, and when Claude is deployed to Vietnam, Berger goes in his place and dies there—all because, for a few minutes, he pretended to be somebody he was not.

To be honest, the story gave me a sick feeling. By the end, I was in such a state that I left during the credits, whispering to Donny— even though he looked annoyed—that I would meet him in the lobby...where I hastily bought two boxes of chocolate peanut butter malt balls to calm my nerves and a large Diet Pepsi. I was just starting the second box of malt balls when I heard my name.

"Zelda!" shrieked Dorothy Gilhooley, pulling Ralph's arm as she spotted me in front of the concession stand. "Zelda, what a surprise to see you here. What a silly movie. I dragged Ralph here to see Peter Sellers, and then *that* came on. I just don't know what to think. All those bare-bottomed hippies. How *are* you? I heard you finally got a car."

"Hi, Dorothy," I answered, praying Donny would stay in the theatre. "How nice to see you both. Yes, I guess that was pretty silly."

"A bunch of fags, the whole lot," sneered Ralph.

"Ralph, language," said Dorothy, blushing. "Ralph was a Red Beret."

"Green. Green. How many times do I have to tell you?" snarled Ralph, his face beet red.

"Tone," said Dorothy in the voice she used with unruly students.

Ralph's face scared me, but Dorothy didn't seem to notice as she cozied up to me, asking more questions about my car as though it were the most fascinating thing that had ever happened in Moose Country.

"It's just a used one," I explained, seeing Donny coming out of the theatre in my peripheral vision. Please, God, let him see the situation before he—

"Miss McFigg! Mr. and Mrs. Gilhooley!" he exclaimed, coming over. "What a surprise to see you all." And he had such a sincere look of surprise that I almost believed him. "That was some movie, huh?"

"Shit," said Ralph.

"Language!" exclaimed Dorothy.

"Donny!" said I with as much surprise as I could exude. "What a lovely surprise. Where is your grandfather? So nice to see you. Is he picking you up?"

"No, he's busy this afternoon," said Donny forlornly, knowing exactly where I was going with this. "I've got to walk home."

"Oh," said Dorothy, stepping on my next line. "We'd be happy to—" but Ralph elbowed her with such force that it looked as if he cracked a rib. "Oh dear me," said Dorothy, trying to act as if he hadn't just brutalized her.

"Don't you remember we've got the thing this afternoon," said Ralph with a smile that made my stomach drop. "Don't you remember, sweetheart?"

Dorothy looked mortified. "Oh, of course, the thing."

"Donny, can I give you a ride home?" said I congenially.

"Okay," said Donny with the same look of genuine surprise and vulnerability as before. "If you really don't mind."

"Not at all," said I.

Ralph scowled and glanced at his watch. Then, giving us a cursory wave, he turned away, practically dragging Dorothy toward the exit. "I ain't taking no Injun in my—" he said just loud enough for us to hear it, and Dorothy went white.

"Please wait for me in the car," she said, pulling away from him. "I'll be there in a minute." Ralph looked like he wanted to yank her arm off, but he deferred, shoving open the lobby door and striding out into the parking lot.

As soon as he was gone, Dorothy threw out her arms and hurried back to us. "I'm so sorry," she said imploringly to Donny. "I'm so—"

"Hey," said Donny, holding up one hand to stop her. "You don't have to."

"Oh, but I do," said Dorothy, near tears. "So many bad things have happened to you, and I want you to know that they aren't your fault."

"I know that," said Donny.

"No," said Dorothy. "No, you don't. You have to know that *none* of them are your fault. Not Mr. Gilhooley, not your grandfather, and certainly not Mrs. Lagerfelt, bless her heart, the poor crazy thing."

I leaned forward, but Donny grabbed me by the back of my waistband and pulled. "It's okay, Mrs. Gilhooley, you really don't have to say these things," said Donny.

"Oh, yes I do," continued Dorothy. "You need to know you are a beautiful young man, and it's not your fault if a mentally unstable woman acts so wicked. It was right for you to say no. You did the right thing telling. She'll get the help she needs now, and nobody blames you for it. And no doubt Mrs. Lagerfelt herself will one day thank you. I can't imagine how difficult it must have been having a woman of her authority make such ridiculous and vindictive accusations. But I hope you'll find it in your heart to forgive her. Mrs. Lagerfelt, bless her heart, has a history of sexual delusions. Last year she was sure the entire eighth grade football team was after her, and she turned this place upside down when Principal Appleton suggested she take a sabbatical. It was just a matter of time."

Donny drove us back to my house. I'd intended to, but once in the driver's seat, I was overcome with such exhaustion that I was unable to turn the ignition key. Donny drove slowly, making full stops at all the back-roads stop signs even though there was no traffic. As we passed the school, we both turned our heads to the parking lot. No cars. As we passed Lurleen Lagerfelt's house, neither of us turned.

According to the Vermont weather bureau, winter ends at the spring equinox in late March, but everything in Moose Country was still frozen. I'd wondered if Donny had buried his grandfather's remains before the ground got too hard, but, per our agreement, I never asked.

There was an old dog lying in the middle of the frozen road. Donny saw him and slowed to a turtle's pace, circling wide. The dog didn't even look up.

You'd think Moose Country folk would be churchgoing, but this was not the case. There was only one Congregational Church with a congregation that had dwindled to a few elderly people with nowhere else to go during holidays. I don't know what people did on Sundays, but from the cars and pickups in driveways and the lack of movie audience at the mall, it was clear they stayed home.

"Of all the people to run into at the movies," was all I said as Donny pulled up in front of my gate cabin.

Donny stared straight ahead through the windshield at the stunted Azalea bushes in front of my front window. I'd put red bows on them at Christmastime and I'd forgotten to take them off. "Can I ask you a favor?" he said suddenly.

"I guess," I answered. "It seems I owe you."

"Promise you'll get me through high school."

"Sure," I said, with no idea what I was committing to. "Now can I ask you a question?"

"Sure," said Donny.

"Did you sleep with her?"

Donny looked at me and laughed, his black eyes sparkling like the mica boulders on the dirt road to his house. "You have got to be joking!"

"See you tomorrow," said I.

"See ya," said Donny, and he took off in my car.

Chapter 19

Even though I'd bought a television for the express purpose of having an Oscar party, I found myself alone, flicking channels the night of the Academy Awards. The only reason I'd wanted to watch was to see if anyone I knew from off-off-Broadway or temp jobs was in the audience, but still I was pretty shocked to see Mike the poet on one of my flick-throughs. Somebody at the podium was joking with Jack Nicholson in the audience, and there, right beside him, was Mike. He'd cleaned up a lot but was still wearing his signature baseball cap so that anybody who remembered the *Ed Sullivan Show* would recognize him, and he was glad-handing Jack like they were good buddies.

"Hey!" I yelled. "Hey, Mike the poet, you asshole! Boy, if I—" and that's when I felt it. The vacuum. Here I was, alone in a gate cabin at the end of a dead-end road at the bottom of a private driveway to an unoccupied house on the tundra in Vermont, yelling to nobody. I had nobody. No friends from the past. Nobody but Donny, who knew my past, and not even he knew the whole story. There was nobody to phone and say, "Hey, guess who I just saw on the Academy Awards?" because I had no ties, no connections, no roots.

And suddenly I wondered about my mother. Was she alive? Was she still drunk? Did she ever think about me? Did she even try to find me after I left? And what about my father? Had he remarried? Did I have half-siblings somewhere?

For a moment, I envisioned dialing my old number to see if my mother would answer. But almost as fast as the picture arose, it shattered into a million lethally sharp pieces from my next thought: I didn't like my mother. I never had. And she had never liked me. People say that parents love their children, as if it's inevitable. I am living proof that it is not. So, no, I would not phone that person who used to be my mother.

The person I wanted to phone was a caring older woman who'd been so distraught at my disappearance that she'd rallied the CIA, the FBI, and the National Guard to root me out. The person I wanted to phone would have been so overcome with remorse about neglecting me that she would have sworn off booze and dedicated her life to making amends. If she couldn't find me, she would be feeding orphans and sending shoes to shoeless kids in India. She would have called my father, who, in a fit of panic, would have posted my photo on billboards and milk cartons. I would have been so sought that I'd have gone underground, living on the kindness of social workers and pimps. The person I wanted to call to say, "Hey, you'll never guess who I just saw on the Academy Awards," was a person who did not exist.

I wondered what it would be like to have such people to call. Come to think of it, I'll bet there were plenty of them inside those Moose Country homes with cars and pickups parked in driveways. I'll bet there were people who would be worried sick if their kids disappeared. I'll bet they even did bed checks during the night and said things like, "What would you like for dinner?" I'll bet if I were to look in those homes, I would see comfortable living rooms with sideboards and dark wood crockery cabinets that had been passed down from parents and great grandparents. There would be kitchens stocked with cookies and Popsicles and things kids liked to eat. The basements would be converted playrooms full of ping-pong tables and HO train sets, with rolling farmscapes populated by red silos and toy farmers with miniature livestock. Little toy farm wives in pinafore aprons would be standing on porches ringing tiny farm bells to call the boys in for supper.

I'll bet supper in Moose Country homes was a sit-down affair where moms and dads asked kids what happened at school that day and said things like, "How are you?"

As I mentioned, I was sitting alone in a gate cabin at the end of a dead end. When I'd first moved in, I'd used my bobby pin to gain entrance to the Montavaldo mansion at the end of the private driveway at the top of the hill, and quite frankly it was a disappointment. After several hours of walking from room to room, examining the contents of bureaus and cabinets and closets and reading some personal mail, I snacked on some canned tuna, concluding that the contents of my gate cabin were far more interesting. But I did wonder what I'd find in the homes up the street—those homes with bright porch lights and unlocked back doors. It was just a thought.

Mike the poet was leaning toward Jack Nicholson to hear a comment that Jack would never tell anyone but a best buddy. Then Mike laughed, slapping his thighs with such vigor that you'd never believe he once lived in a fleabag hotel where he puked in the hall.

When the show was over, I wrote him a letter:

> *Dear Mike,*
> *I saw you on the Academy Awards with*
> *Jack Nicholson. You looked like you were*
> *having a great time. I'm still waiting for*

the stipend and the rent I had to pay at the
Embassy Hotel before José would let me
into our room to get my stuff. Boy, are you
a piece of work. But anyway, I'm glad you
got sober—are you?—and are having great
times with Jack Nicholson.

Sincerely,
Zelda McFigg

P.S. By the way, I had my students—I'm
a teacher now—do a recitation of "Dusty
Rose" in our Christmas play. Everybody
booed.

Because there were no computers yet and no way to Google
an address, I sent my letter to Mike the Poet, c/o The Academy
Awards, Los Angeles, California. I put the envelope in my mailbox
with the flag up—dressed in a red Christmas bow from my Azalea
bush. I didn't get letters and, since I'd never sent any, I wanted to
make sure the postman noticed there was something inside.

Chapter 20

Nobody had signed up for the *Middle School Mutterer*, and Appleton was on my case to publish the debut issue of the newspaper. The lead story was to be an interview with him about the impending merger of the middle school with the new high school—an adjoining pinwheel of brick tentacles that was nearing completion after seven years of construction waylaid by floods, broken sewer pipes, and pestilence.

"Donny," I pleaded, "I need student writers. Just write anything. Don't worry about how it sounds. I'll edit it. It's a student paper. It'll look good on your record."

Donny considered this. We were in his garden. I'd driven over to get my car back after several weeks of asking and hearing excuses about Donny having to take the school bus due to a sudden discomfort about driving without a license—a new concern since our inadvertent car swap.

"Just tell me you'll do it," I pushed. "And then give me my car. Where is it anyway?"

"I busted it," said Donny with a sheepish smile. "I drove it into a tree. I'm really sorry."

"You what?!"

"It's behind the shack," said Donny, pointing up the hill. "I guess I had too much beer."

"Donny!" I exclaimed. "How? Why? Beer?!"

Donny shrugged and smiled some more.

"What is wrong with you? That's my car. Do you want to end up like your grandfather? Why the hell were you drinking beer?"

"I like the taste," he said simply. "Keep my car. I don't care. I'll buy a new one when I turn seventeen. Hey, I got an idea."

"What?" I asked, suddenly giving up. If Donny was determined to become another stereotypical drunk Indian, there was nothing I could do about it. I should have known better than to get so close. Everybody's a disappointment. How could I have been so stupid?

"You write whatever you want for the newspaper and just put my name on it," said Donny brightly. "We both win."

"Fine," I said. "Whatever you want." I turned to walk to my wrecked car.

"Hey, Zelda," he said blocking my path. "Don't be like that. I was kidding. Lighten up, will you? I don't drink all the time. I was low and missed my grampa, so I finished off his stash. To tell you the truth, I hated it. I'm really sorry I wrecked your car. Please, Zelda, I was kidding."

"Really?"

"Yes! God, I can't believe you'd think I'm that stupid."

"Okay," I said, stepping back to see him from a distance. "It's just the history, you know? My mother, your grandfather. It's such an old road."

"Listen," said Donny, standing square in front of me. "Look at me. Do I look like an idiot?"

"No," I said, blushing at his muscleman pose.

"The only thing that would really mess me up is if you gave up on me, Zelda. Promise me that you'll never do that."

"Okay," said I. "I promise."

And so began our collaboration.

Chapter 21

When Donny turned seventeen, I went with him to buy his car, a shiny red pickup truck with an engine rebuilt for free by Ralph Gilhooley, who found Christ after a night of heavy drinking and must have felt guilty about his former bigotry. I signed for Donny's loan and gave him five hundred dollars and his first tank of gas.

Peggy Smithson was not happy going out in a pickup, but Donny teased her relentlessly about being like the spoiled "valley girls" so popular in TV comedy sketches, and she finally gave in.

Peggy and Donny were a popular couple. By eighth grade graduation, she towered over me at a graceful five foot seven; she had porcelain skin and model good looks that earned her the place of head cheerleader as well as anything else she set her mind on—which, rumor had it, included many awards as the region's top young equestrian, but she never talked about her accomplishments, or, in fact, anything she did outside of school. Occasionally, when she didn't seem to know anyone was looking, I noticed a sadness behind those brilliant turquoise eyes, but I never said anything to her. You see, except for our mutual connection with Donny (who had a talent for compartmentalizing confidences and never spoke to me of her or vice versa), Peggy and I had little communication. I respected her privacy...as she respected mine.

By ninth grade, Donny was earning accolades as the darkly handsome six-foot-one-inch editor-in-chief of the school paper—especially following his article on the new high school. He had taped the interview with Appleton, which I then transcribed, edited, and revised into a charming, newsy, slice-of-New England-life piece. Appleton was so delighted that he sent it to the Moose Country Chamber of Commerce, which put it in their newsletter. Which is where the Associated Press discovered it, resulting in its reprint across the country as a "here's what's happening in small-town schools" piece that put the term "brick octopus" into the vernacular (meaning any sprawling, ill-conceived architectural abomination—the definition of which was lost on Appleton, who swooned during the fifteen minutes the photo of him in his tool belt went national).

As a freshman editor-in-chief of a school paper with national attention—which title was changed to *Moose Country Mutterer* to accommodate the high school—Donny bylined award-winning articles on the impact of new gun laws on a population of young hunters whose families survived winters on frozen moose meat; the importance of hot school lunches in Northern New England; and, most famously, in his senior year, an endearing profile of Peggy Smithson entitled "Annals of a Vermont Fashionista."

What was most remarkable about our collaboration was how unremarkable it was. Because of the paper's popularity, there were plenty of student reporters, but none of them noticed that I wrote and Donny had the byline. If I needed to do an interview, Donny made the call and I listened in as his faculty advisor—prompting questions, as necessary, always recording the conversations so I would have the raw material. If a piece required in-person research, Donny would do the visit, then I'd grill him, eliciting details and making up whatever he didn't notice or couldn't remember. Occasionally Donny would actually write a piece that I would then rewrite into life, but we both agreed the original method was more efficient. "What a team we are!" I'd say to him laughing. Our secret gave us an intimacy even closer than girlfriend/boyfriend. We couldn't believe we were getting away with it, and it never occurred to either of us that it might end badly.

Chapter 22

Lurleen Lagerfelt was never the same after her mental hospital incarceration. Apparently she had sealed her fate by blurting, "I slept with him!" in protest of Donny's explanation that her vindictive utterings were those of a woman spurned.

She lost her counseling and teaching licenses but avoided jail time when, after a month on Lithium, she recanted, explaining that she'd been in a depression-induced delusion.

I have no idea how she subsisted after getting out of the facility. I hadn't seen her since the day she was carted away. So it goes without saying that I was surprised to get a call from Lagerfelt nearly five years after the incident asking me to tea.

"I'm concerned about Templeton," she told me over a plate of gingerbread and chocolate chip cookies. (Of course the boy's name is not Templeton, but for the sake of consistency and because I cannot see him as anything but a rat, I will continue the pseudonym.) "I'm afraid he is suffering from sexual dysfunction, body dysmorphia, and borderline personality disorder. Please, Zelda, have a cookie."

Although the cookies looked luscious, I was suddenly gripped by the notion that I had been invited to this tea party for "Lagerfelt's

Revenge" and that the sweets were laced with arsenic. "Thanks," I said, "but I'm watching my waistline."

"Oh, pshaw," said Lagerfelt.

I was momentarily speechless. I had never heard anybody actually say the word "pshaw." "No, really," I protested. "I'm on very strict diet."

"You eat like a bird," said Lagerfelt, stuffing a whole chocolate chip cookie into her mouth. "In my experience, men like a woman with cushioning."

Perhaps it was only the gingerbread that were poisoned. "Well, if you insist," I said, carefully choosing a chocolate chip from the bottom of the stack.

"Good," said Lagerfelt, sighing deeply. "Now the point is, Templeton is padding his crotch."

"Excuse me?" I replied. The cookie was very good, and I wanted to eat several more, but the conversation was taking an uncomfortable turn. "He's doing what to his what?" I asked, picking through the pile for the largest chocolate chips.

"Oh, please, Zelda. Can't we be professional about this? It's a cry for help. Something must be done. Attention must be paid. We're both professionals, aren't we?"

Now I was sure—she'd discovered my nonexistent teaching credentials and had poisoned the gingerbread. I would have to be very, very careful with my responses. "Of course, we're both professionals. Now why do you think the boy is padding his penis?"

Lagerfelt's face settled into a serious expression. "Self-esteem issues."

"Ah," I said, nodding in agreement.

"But we must keep this confidential. If he knew we knew, it would crush him."

"Of course," I answered. I really prefer milk with my chocolate chip cookies, but to avoid extra conversation, I washed them down with tea. In case Lagerfelt was insane, it would be best to eat, then politely excuse myself after an acceptable tea party interval. "So.... How do you know?" I asked with a sudden inspiration: if she knew because she was sleeping with students again, perhaps I could get something on her to derail any attempts to discredit me and ruin my perfect life.

In my opinion, my life in Moose Country *was* perfect. Although I knew nothing about education, I seemed to have a gift for teaching. After five years, I had developed a popular curriculum, integrating dramatic presentation with children's and young adult literature, plus whatever else caught my fancy. Using Mrs. Freeman's notes, which I discovered mid-way through my first year, I covered grammar basics, vocabulary, and composition. And utilizing my background as an off-off-Broadway thespian, I was a most effective instructor in the art of oral communication *avec* music and movement when I was so inspired and Mrs. Lambert was in the mood to play the piano.

As I mentioned earlier, the school newspaper was a raving success, and after the media coverage, being a reporter became popular to the point that I had to turn down students. Donny used his position as editor-in-chief to his best advantage, becoming a darling of the Chamber of Commerce who welcomed the opportunity to showcase a young Abenaki Indian on their promotional literature, giving the impression that Moose Country was a progressive, politically correct community that rich city folk would feel good about investing in.

Donny was a terrific boy, a good friend, and over the years we'd found a mutually comfortable rhythm with one another, as well as with Peggy Smithson. We each had our role. By senior year, Donny was six foot three and arrestingly handsome, so he was the hub of our triumvirate of secret-keepers. Peggy was the beautiful girlfriend/helpmate, and I was the mentor/friend. I was steadfast in my presentation as faculty advisor, but, *entre nous*, I loved the boy. I was only six and a half years older, and due to the underdevelopment of my dating and sex skills, I frequently was Donny's student. Where somebody of more experience might have offered anecdotes and advice, I cleverly masked my inexperience, simultaneously enhancing my "good teacher" persona, by being a good and silent listener. To tell you the truth, on some level I'm sure I envied Lurleen Lagerfelt's sexual exploits, but I was determined not to let her know.

"It was the bulge," she said. "I saw it through Templeton's costume during the senior play. He is obviously compensating."

I'd had no idea she was attending my productions. She must have slipped out right after curtain. The last play I'd cast Templeton in was Mr. Arthur Miller's *Death of a Salesman*. I knew it was risky casting, but honestly the boy did a mean Willy Loman, using his shortness as motivation for his eventual suicide. "He was wearing loose-fitting beige suit pants," I replied. "Perhaps you are mistaken."

Lagerfelt solemnly shook her head. "Zelda, I know what I saw."

"Well, what would you suggest I do?" I queried. This was absurd. So what if the boy had enlarged his crotch; what difference did it make in the grand scheme of things? But I held my tongue, respectfully awaiting Lagerfelt's advice.

"I would be willing to see him for private counseling, strictly as a lay therapist," said Lagerfelt, sitting back in her chair and cradling her teacup. "It would be nontraditional talk therapy—I've been studying with an Ecuadorian shaman—and I'd charge on a sliding scale, depending on what his parents can afford. I was hoping, considering our history, that you might recommend this. Of course, there is no need to mention his padded crotch to his parents. You could just say that you thought their son might benefit from some self-esteem counseling."

It had been fifteen minutes—a sufficient amount of time for a tea party, in my estimation—so I excused myself and said that I would certainly give the matter serious contemplation. I said I was not in the habit of recommending psychological counseling, as that was not my area of expertise, but, yes, I would consider it. Lagerfelt said she certainly hoped so, considering our mutual history, and she walked me to the door.

Even in her demented, cookie-drugged state, Lagerfelt's eyes had a drilling quality, so when I got home, I took a shower and put on clean everything. Then, to clear my head, I walked up the long, private driveway to the Montavaldo mansion.

It was late fall 1987, and the Montavaldos hadn't been up for two seasons, so I felt comfortable using my bobby pin to gain entrance and make myself comfortable in the big family room. I lay down on one of the overstuffed sofas and contemplated the floral print and my predicament.

On one hand, I did not feel good about having allowed Donny to destroy Lagerfelt's life. Her husband had divorced her shortly after she was released from the mental hospital, and I could certainly understand how she might need some extra income. But on the other hand, none of this was my fault. I had merely been seen touching Donny's shoulder in a VW bug. I did not cause Lagerfelt's destruction. I did not make her demented.

But on the other hand, the woman *was* demented and it was not beyond comprehension that she blamed me and would try to destroy me if I did not help her get a therapy client.

What to do?

This was too much to contemplate on an empty stomach, so I moseyed into the white marble kitchen with stainless steel fixtures and restaurant ovens to see what nonperishables I might find in the walk-in pantry. Tomorrow I would start a yogurt diet. Only one hundred calories a serving.

Chapter 23

Because Donny was older than his classmates, senior year he turned twenty. "I'm going to tell everybody that my grampa died," he announced the day after his birthday. It was a freezing late-October day and we were in my classroom washing the board, as was our decompressing custom after the closing bell. "What do you think?" he asked, wringing out the sponge and starting another top-to-bottom stroke.

I loved to watch Donny wash. The way he stretched and pulled with such surety and accuracy, leaving smooth, clean chalkboard in his wake. "I think that's a fine idea," I answered. "What are you going to do for a body?"

Donny shrugged. "I'll think of something. I always do."

"I wish this place had a fireplace," I grumbled. Despite my heaviest sweater and silk long underwear, I could not get warm, and I was in a cranky mood. "Lurleen Lagerfelt wants me to tell Templeton's parents that they should send him to her for therapy on account of he's padding his crotch."

Donny stopped mid-stroke and stared at me, incredulous.

"I'm not making this up. She invited me over for tea and may have even poisoned the cookies."

"Zelda, you're out of your mind," said Donny, and he resumed washing.

I had told Donny several bits of my history—about my time with Mike the poet and my off-off-Broadway work—but I may have left out the fact that I had no teaching credentials. I'd assumed he knew, but he'd never asked. I suddenly felt so tired I feared I might fall down, and it was all I could do to get to my chair.

"Are you worried she's going to hurt you if you don't do what she wants?" asked Donny with his back to me.

"Yes," I sighed.

"I'll take care of it," said Donny.

"Okay," said I. "Okay."

I'd learned over the course of our friendship that it was best not to ask for details when it came to Donny's activities. I still had no idea where he'd buried his grampa, and when he told me that Lurleen Lagerfelt had arranged for his grampa's funeral at the Congregational Church on the second Sunday in November, I simply said, "What time should I be there?"

"I told them he was cremated," said Donny. "Twelve o'clock."

The Moose Country Congregational Church was a small white stucco building with two stained glass windows and twelve rows of dark wood pews. The church held a lot of funerals due to the fact that the average congregant was an octogenarian. Apparently they were dying off fast, and the crowd for funerals was drastically diminished with each new death.

There was a strange gap between Moose Country's elderly and the rabidly copulating generation of non-churchgoers. It was as if the elderly had bore no offspring, causing a missing generation of people in their fifties and sixties—except for Dorothy and Ralph Gilhooley who were transplants from Texas. Perhaps the copulating parents of my students migrated here like me—as if pulled into the vortex of the absent generation. Perhaps that's how Lurleen Lagerfelt had landed here.

There was not a big crowd for Grampa Sherman's service. Just the few Moose Country faculty who couldn't think fast enough to come up with an excuse, Peggy Smithson's family, and three grim looking Native American men who stood behind the last pew even though there were plenty of empty seats.

"We are gathered here to celebrate the life of Jeremy Turn Bull Sherman," said the young minister, enunciating brightly and projecting to the wall behind the Indians. "Unfortunately, I did not have the pleasure of knowing Jeremy, but his grandson, Donny Sherman, would like to say a few words, after which, we invite any friends of Jeremy to share their thoughts and memories. Donny?"

And with that, Donny rose from his seat and stepped up on the altar. As always, his was a commanding presence. He cleared his throat nervously, but I knew he would be fine from all of his stage experience, so I relaxed as much as you can in a wooden pew and perused the audience. There were a few elderly people I didn't recognize still dressed in their parkas. There was a dark, very dignified, silver-haired man with a small, fat woman. Both were dressed in heavy wool clothes with bright foreign-looking scarves. They looked Indian, but not like the men at the back of the church. I scanned the row in front of mine, and to my surprise, at the end of it, right on the aisle next to Lurleen Lagerfelt, sat Templeton, and instantly I knew that somehow Donny had taken care of me.

"In conclusion," continued Donny, whose speech I missed in my fascination with the audience, "I'd like to say that my grampa was a drunken, miserable SOB who beat the crap out of me, but I loved him. I'll miss you, Grampa."

There was stunned silence, then the church doors creaked open, letting in a blast of stinging cold, and everyone turned their heads.

"You have lost your soul, son," said the tallest of the grim-faced Indian men. Then he and his two companions exited the church in a cloud of frozen breath.

Nobody offered to come up on the altar to share further thoughts about Grampa Sherman. So the minister said, "Our prayers are with the soul who has left this earth as well as his family." Then he stepped away from the podium, signaling that the service was over.

"Hello, Miss McFigg," said Templeton as we met in the aisle.

"Hello, dear," I answered, willing myself to keep my focus on his face. "Hello, Mrs. Lagerfelt," I said as she stepped to his side.

"I really appreciate the opportunity, Miss McFigg," said Templeton. "Donny told me you recommended me. I promise you won't be sorry."

"Ah," I said. This could not be good. "Well, I'm certain you'll do very well. Nice to see you, Mrs. Lagerfelt. Forgive me, but I must run." And as fast as my girth would allow, I made my way down the aisle, out of the church, to my car.

Not good, not good at all, I thought as I turned the ignition of my cold engine. I had a scream lodged in my throat and flapping bats in my stomach as I pumped the gas pedal until the engine finally caught and I sped out of the church lot. What had Donny done now?

"I thought you'd be happy," protested Donny. "He's going to her for counseling. Isn't that what you wanted?"

"But not as a spy for the newspaper," I answered. "This is insane, Donny. We can't publish an exposé of Lurleen Lagerfelt."

"We won't publish it," said Donny incredulously. "Do you think I'm crazy?"

It was dusk, the day after the funeral, and Donny had come over to my house after school to get my emergency signature on some documents. One was an overdue financial aid thing and the others, I didn't really know. Several years ago, just in case Donny had been discovered living alone and under-age, he had asked me to co-sign some papers that I was now un-signing. There seemed to be a tacit agreement among the Moose Country powers that be that even though Donny was only twenty, he would be accepted as an adult. Although I doubt that any of it was legal—my signing or my un-signing—since we had no witnesses, I was happy to do anything to help Donny feel more secure. He'd come to my house to assume responsibility for all things having to do with his life and possessions now that his grampa was legally dead.

"But you told Templeton he was doing an investigative story for the paper. How can you have him get his parents to pay for therapy, then not use what he writes?"

Donny smiled sheepishly and shrugged. "Stuff happens, Zelda. Hey, don't forget to initial my change on the last page."

"Done," I said, scribbling ZM and handing him the papers. "What is he supposed to be looking for anyway?"

"Whatever there is," said Donny simply. "I left it up to him."

"Investigative reporter," I said with disdain.

"He likes the title, and besides, all the TV stations have them," said Donny, almost laughing. "His parents are psyched. They've got their heart set on Yale, and they can probably still slide this onto his application. Mrs. Lagerfelt even wrote him a recommendation, so, see, there's another benefit."

"I don't know, Donny," said I. "I just don't know."

Chapter 24

Like many people in small-town America, Lurleen Lagerfelt means well. She always has. Like many professionals in rural environments, she has cultivated her little patch of the American dream by hanging out a professional shingle: Psychological Counselor. Counting on word-of-mouth and small-town ignorance, she hopes to attract a lucrative crop of neurotics in need who will not question her methods or competence.

In November of 1987, our sessions began— as this reporter would have expected—with Mrs. Lagerfelt asking why I had come. As I was there in my capacity as an investigative reporter (unbeknownst to my kind, hard-working, indulgent, and somewhat oblivious parents who thought I had self-esteem issues—Sorry, Mom and Dad), I was not completely forthcoming. I chose to present myself as a normal adolescent boy with normal adolescent concerns such as being popular and fitting in. Since adolescence, by definition, is the period of life when one grapples with rapid growth and the concurrent hormones and emotions, in this reporter's opinion, there was nothing presented that required psychological counseling. Nevertheless, Mrs. Lagerfelt prescribed a course of treatment that began with conversation:

Me: Sometimes I'm shy.

Mrs. L: How do you feel about that?

Me: Lousy.

Mrs. L: What does lousy feel like?

Which conversation was followed by me lying on the floor while Mrs. L performed a ritual drum and whistling routine, apparently taught to her by a witch doctor. She then cracked raw eggs over me, after which I handed over payment for the session from my parents.

After four months of "treatment," it is this reporter's opinion that Lurleen Lagerfelt's actions were by any stretch of the imagination unethical and probably indicate some level of self-delusion or insanity. Contrary to rumor, Mrs. Lagerfelt did not appear to be a nymphomaniac, although in all honesty, this reporter might not have kicked her out of bed.

"Oh my God, Donny," I groaned, dropping the manuscript on the floor, like the filth that it was.

"Hey, she wrote him a college recommendation, so she was okay with the whole thing. All he told his parents about was the investigative reporter title. He can still spit out some crap about school lunches, he's amazingly fast, and—*kazam*—everyone's happy."

"Everyone but the lunch ladies."

"Zelda, Zelda, Zelda, you're overthinking this."

"Does Lurleen *know*?"

"Of course not. I just said she wrote him a college recommendation. You're not listening! We're not gonna publish it. Will you please relax?"

I leaned back on the tufted blue sofa and closed my eyes. Then I opened them and stared at the ugly faux-wood paneled walls which Ralph Gilhooley had promised Principal Appleton would look like the real thing. After the Chamber of Commerce had gotten interested in the newspaper, Appleton decided that the *Moose Country Mutterer* should have a professional office where visiting AP reporters would feel comfortable. The dark plastic paneling made a nice background for photos of students writing stories and Appleton posing as the benign tzar of progressive education.

"He'll never get into Yale," I said, slipping off my shoes and examining my swollen toes. Ever since the new dress code, following the new newspaper office renovation of the old home ec. room, my feet hurt.

"I'll get him in," said Donny, casually putting his feet up on the story file and leaning back in his editor-in-chief's swivel chair.

"Yeah, right," I said. "With your grades—"

"I got in," said Donny, yawning off-handedly.

"Excuse me?" I said.

"I got into Yale," said Donny glibly. "I heard a few months ago. Early decision. Being a token Indian editor-in-chief apparently trumps the grade thing."

"Donny!" I shrieked. "Oh my God, why didn't you tell me? Oh my God, this is wonderful."

"Full scholarship," he mumbled, scratching his chin. "Just got that news. Was late on my financial aid forms. Thanks for signing them, by the way."

"Holy crap! Holy crap!" I really needed to lose some weight. I fell back on the couch, gasping. "I—I—I—"

"Easy there, Zelda," said Donny in his soothing voice. "It's just school."

An interview wasn't necessary for Donny. He was unequivocally accepted. But he had till mid-May to accept and he was invited to an early-decision spring tea with his college dean. Yale University was divided into twelve residential colleges where students lived and ate and went to the library and had parties where they met people who would later get them jobs and entrée into exclusive boardrooms and country clubs. Each college had its own master and dean. The masters were administrators, and the deans were personal advisors.

Donny was to be at his dean's residence in Trumbull College at twelve o'clock the following sunny Sunday. I was driving, and it was a full car: me as Donny's mentor; Templeton to take a tour, be introduced to the dean, and to be buttered up by Donny before he learned that we were not going to publish the product of four months of research and hundreds of his parents' dollars; and Peggy Smithson because Donny had insisted.

I was worried about getting lost, but it turned out the bigger problem was my homicidal urges. For five mind-numbing hours, we drove straight south on I-91, and I thought if Peggy said she had to pee one more time, or if Templeton repeated "Are we there yet?" in a little kid's voice which he apparently thought was hilarious, or if Donny addressed me once more as "Miss McFigg," I might wreck the car simply to shut them up and alleviate the boredom. But finally we arrived.

"If I'd known I'd be stuck in a stinky car for five friggin hours, I wouldn't have come," announced Peggy as she pushed open the door. "What is this, a friggin castle? Is this where you're going to live, Donny? Why don't you get a place off campus so at least we can have some privacy when I visit? God, my skirt is all wrinkled. Where is the bathroom?"

Donny put his arm around Peggy, and wordlessly our disgruntled group approached the dungeon door entrance to what looked like a fortress.

Inside the doors, we found a large grassy courtyard where a couple of kids were tossing a Frisbee and others were reading.

"A bunch of spoiled jocks," said Templeton. "I'd like to bomb the place."

"What a joker," said Donny, tousling his hair. Then, calling to the Frisbee kids, he asked, "Can you tell us where the dean's residence is?"

Donny was a remarkable young man. I never tired of watching people's first reactions to his open, boyish smile and his twinkly eyes. People liked him immediately, and, thinking back, it was almost inconceivable that it had ever been otherwise. If asked about the days when they had taunted him for being overweight, I'm sure his Moose Country classmates would have been incredulous, swearing that it never happened.

I, on the other hand, still battled first impressions. People did not automatically like me. I'm sure they saw me as pathetic, and my physique as repulsive no matter how carefully I put myself together. Even before the success of the newspaper and Appleton's dress code, I had begun taking great care with my wardrobe and makeup and deodorant application. There is an assumption that fat people are sloppy and smelly, and since, in my case, the latter had some merit, I dedicated two hours every morning to a tidy and odorless presentation.

This morning I had begun my ablutions at five A.M., as we needed to be on the road by seven. For makeup, I had opted for neat, natural color over a heavy foundation, the weight of which gave me a mature, authoritative look. For costume, I had selected a loose-fitting green knit skort and top ensemble that I hoped would appear fresh even after five hours at the wheel of a VW bug, chauffeuring three insolent high school seniors, two of whom made my hair follicles hurt. I was determined to appear professional yet maternal when we met Donny's dean. It was important that Donny have a solid support system for his introduction into the Ivy League—particularly since his entire school newspaper career was a sham.

"Ah, you brought the tribe!" said Dean Pruitt, and then he blushed, realizing the political incorrectness of using the word "tribe" to a person of Native ancestry.

"Can't get rid of the posse," joked Donny, enveloping Peggy on one side and Templeton, who disappeared into his armpit, on the other. And he laughed in such a friendly, open way that Dean Pruitt relaxed and reached for his hand.

"Will you join me for drinks and snacks in my office?" he invited, gesturing us down a real wood-paneled hall to a door on the right.

We were in the dean's residence and I could hear children in the background. The man was not young. Perhaps he had married a fertile student—a former undergrad who became enamored with his authority and sophisticated demeanor, mistaking both for power.

I gave the marriage one more year—until she realized her husband was a glorified babysitter.

"We have caramelized onion brie *en croutes*, crab cakes, and lamb kibbeh on warm pita bread," said Dean Pruitt, pointing to a setting of sterling silver platters on his sideboard. "And please help yourselves to drinks. You must be parched after the drive."

Donny, Templeton, and Peggy crowded around the sideboard filling their plates, while I held back, observing as a mentor should.

"Miss McFigg?" said Dean Pruitt, "won't you have something to eat?"

I knew he was thinking, *What a pig, she'll probably eat the whole platter of lamb kibbeh*, so to foil him, I said, "Yes, thank you. I'm waiting for the children to finish." And when they did, I put one crab cake on my plate and filled a crystal goblet with Diet Pepsi.

"What a thoughtful spread," I gushed, sitting demurely on the couch to observe my students, who surrounded his desk, awaiting words of wisdom.

"So how was the trip?" asked Dean Pruitt, looking directly at Donny.

"Boring for me," said Donny, "although for Templeton here, it will probably turn into a Pulitzer Prize-winning news feature. He's our investigative reporter."

"Oh?" said Dean Pruitt, looking at Templeton with interest. "Do you work on the *Moose Country Mutterer* also? Such a delightful title."

"Yes, delightfully," said Templeton with a barely suppressed smirk. "It's a delightful job, mine. I've just done a piece on our former quack guidance counselor."

"Really?" said Dean Pruitt. "Tell me more."

"A wonderful piece!" I interjected before he could utter Lagerfelt's name. "Such a pity that we've had to kill it."

Templeton's face froze, then a look of hate filled his eyes, and I thanked God for my impulse to take the blame. Donny would need Templeton's friendship. I would not. "I'm so sorry, Templeton," I said, exuding matriarchal kindness. "I'm afraid this is rather awkward, Dean Pruitt. Templeton did not know. I only had a chance to review the piece last night, and I'm afraid, for legal reasons—libel and such—we won't be able to run it. But it is first-rate journalism— really on a par with Donny's. I was hoping that might influence the admissions people when they consider Templeton's application."

"Oh, so you're applying to Yale also?" said Dean Pruitt, trying to be polite.

"We're a team," said Donny before Templeton could open his mouth. "My right hand man at the paper. Couldn't do any of it without him."

Pruitt smiled the way adults do when they watch babies being cute. "And you, young lady? Are you applying to Yale as well?" he said, turning to Peggy.

Peggy took her time chewing and swallowing a large bite of onion brie *en croute,* then she wiped her mouth and recrossed her legs, allowing her white cotton skirt to ride up her leg just enough to expose one of her well-developed thighs. "Nope," she said, popping the "p" like a kiss and staring at the dean with a naked, unwavering look.

Dean Pruitt, who may have been a red-head in his youth, blushed crimson as he took a big gulp of tea, burning his mouth but too stunned to acknowledge it. "Excuse me," he said, coughing. "I'll be right back." And he hastily left the room.

"What the hell do you mean, you're killing my piece?" exploded Templeton as soon as Pruitt was out.

My skort had ridden up in back and my legs were sticking to the tufted leather sofa. Also I was ravenously hungry, so I bought time by saying, "Well, now" as I struggled up off the sofa and over to the sterling silver platters. "Mmm, yummy snacks. These crab cakes sure are tasty."

"What the hell?" said Templeton.

Because he seemed on the verge of tears and Peggy had that look she got just before saying something sarcastic, I blurted, "It was my call, Templeton, and I'm sorry, but we can't afford a lawsuit."

"What did you write, anyway?" said Peggy, loosening her ponytail and shaking out her thick blonde hair, slyly ignoring Donny's hand, outreached to touch it.

"Why would *you* care?" said Templeton, imploding with rage. "I just spent four months pretending to be neurotic in order to expose that Lagerfelt quack is all."

"And you did excellent work," said I. "Just superb. It's just that—"

"You're only in danger if you know that the information is false and you publish it with reckless disregard," said Peggy, sounding as if she were reading, and simultaneously admiring the tips of her hair.

"Peggy's going to be a lawyer like her dad," said Donny, smiling as she finally looked at him and their eyes locked.

"This is all very sweet," said Templeton, "but why the hell did you give me the assignment if you didn't want me to call her a quack? She plays drums and whistles for godsake. I want my story published!"

"Fresh-squeezed orange juice!" announced Dean Pruitt, entering with a sterling silver pitcher. "I suddenly realized you all probably haven't had breakfast. My wife's brother sends us crates of oranges every year. He has a farm. Please help yourselves," he said, making space on the sideboard and setting the pitcher down beside the rest of the silver set. "Now, Donny, I saw on your application that you've fenced. I don't know if you know, but Trumbull has an excellent team."

None of us said anything and Donny, who'd complained that sword fighting was for sissies for the entire miserable practice hour when I'd cast him as Mercutio, said, "No, I didn't know. That's super. I'd love to join as long as it doesn't interfere with my studies."

After we'd finished our snacks and beverages, Dean Pruitt stood up and looked at Donny. "I noticed on your application that your middle name is Turn Bull. A funny coincidence there: Did you know that was the original name of Trumbull? The Scotts corrupted it with their rolling 'r's. Ah-ha-ha. Don't suppose you're related to Governor Trumbull—no, of course not. Just joking. So, I'd like to give you the tour, show you where you'll be living."

As Peggy and Templeton stood to go with him, I cleared my throat. "I think it would be best if Peggy, Templeton, and I took a walk. After all, this *is* Donny's visit."

"Certainly," snapped Dean Pruitt, clearly grateful for my intervention, and he escorted Donny to the door. "*Fortuna Favet Audaci!* Fortune Favors the Brave—the Trumbull motto. Hope you're feeling brave, Donny," he said as he clapped my most favorite boy on the shoulder. "See you all at half past." And they were gone.

"'You're only in danger if you know the information is false,'" whined Templeton impersonating Peggy in a simpering falsetto. "Who the hell do you think you are, Clarence Darrow?"

"Hey!" said Peggy, holding up her hand like a policeman.

"So what if it's not all true? The point is the woman is a fruitcake, and if I had to exaggerate a little to make the dramatic truth, so be it. Besides which, since when did you become a champion of the truth, Miss Algebra Genius?"

"Give me a break," said Peggy, tossing her hair back and braiding it into a ponytail. "I'm going to look around. If I were you, I'd do the same. Donny is going to get you into this place for godsake, so stop your bellyaching. Who cares about a stupid high school newspaper article anyway? And you do too need therapy," she said, pointing vaguely at his crotch.

Templeton turned deep red and stomped out the door. Peggy waited for the sound of the front door slamming, then strolled out after him.

I gathered a selection of crab cakes, cheese, and lamb kibbeh on a white china plate. Then, filling my sparkling crystal goblet with fresh-squeezed orange juice, I perused the framed black-and-white photos on the wall behind the sideboard: several of virile Yale sports teams—fencing, crew, lacrosse—featuring a fresh-faced Dean Pruitt with twinkly eyes and a devilish grin. Little did young Pruitt know that in a forty-year blink he'd still be here—chasing this youth through a twenty-five-year-old wife and being put in his place by a girl young enough to be his grandchild. "How time does fly," I may have said out loud as I sipped the juice—mmm, chilled to perfection. Then I sat down on the tufted leather sofa, rolled a napkin under each leg so I wouldn't stick, and I ate.

Chapter 25

I had attended six Moose Country graduations, but the class of eighty-eight was *my* first class, Donny's class—*my* Donny's graduation!

The ceremony was to begin at two o'clock on the football field behind the south and west brick tentacles, set up with a platform and podium where Principal Appleton would call names and Mrs. Lambert would hand out diplomas.

It was a perfect, cloudless, breezy June day. Inspired by three years of listening to that musical abomination in which forty-five overpaid celebrities declared, in song, that they represented the planet's entire population and, thus, people should buy their record and end African hunger, Principal Appleton had decided that graduation would be an opportunity for the fifty-seven seniors to hold hands and sing.

Mrs. Lambert was ecstatic. She took her place at the piano, flouncing her new red taffeta dress and waving her hands about to get the children's attention. Then counting off the beats, she struck a chord and nodded to the linked seniors who sang, not quite in unison, words I dare not quote lest I incur a royalty obligation to people with enough coinage between them to buy Africa and turn it into a country club.

Although I found the anthem insipid, I was moved—mainly by the vision of my Donny standing so tall and strong and open, so happy and proud, despite the fact that he had no family and had severed his connections with the Abenaki Tribal Council, who'd benignly allowed him to stay in his house until he left for college. I could relate to his isolation, sitting as I was next to Dorothy and Ralph Gilhooley, who spat into his handkerchief and checked his watch.

When the song finally ended, Mrs. Lambert bowed and the crowd clapped and hooted enthusiastically. Then Mr. Chuck and several boys from the audio visual club rolled her piano away on its casters, and Mrs. Lambert took her place on the platform.

"Ah-hem," said Principal Appleton, stepping to the podium. "Ah-hem, is this thing on?"

The microphone squealed and Mrs. Lambert shrieked.

"Oh for goodness sake, woman," said Appleton, not realizing he was being amplified. "Ah-hem. Ah, so there we are. Well. I want to welcome you all to the graduation of the class of 1988!"

Applause, hoots. Out of the corner of my eye, I saw a short-haired, very skinny Lurleen Lagerfelt slip into a seat at the end of the row behind mine, and I felt my heart soften. Yes, she was demented, but I believe she had real feeling for my boy. It was good that she had come, but what on earth had she done to her coiffure?

"Many changes have taken place since this class began its journey," intoned Principal Appleton in his best stentorian voice. "The school expanded and gained national recognition through our little newspaper. And I'm proud to announce that a record number of graduates will be going on to colleges and universities and trade schools this year. As you all know, Moose Country values a progressive perspective where students are recognized for more than just numerical evaluations of their academics. Therefore, today's speaker has been chosen by his class to represent the best of our progressive outlook."

Donny shifted, embarrassed, and glanced at Templeton beside him. They were an odd pair. Donny towered over the rat boy. Donny was well-muscled and lean, like a Native American Clark Kent/Superman to Templeton's short, wiry, Cagneyesque Jimmy-the-reporter. But a real friendship had been forged when Donny convinced Dean Pruitt that Templeton's resourcefulness and drive would be such an asset to Yale that the dean had intervened with the admissions office. I felt my little heart skip several beats as Principal Appleton extolled Donny's leadership skills. Templeton looked up at him and smirked. Donny pulled the tassel on his cap, Templeton laughed, and I snuck a glance at Dorothy and Ralph to see if they were appreciating the full magnitude of our accomplishment, but they seemed otherwise engaged.

"So without further adieu," continued Appleton, "it is my honor to present the speaker for the class of eighty-eight, Donny Sherman!" And the crowd erupted in cheers and applause.

Grinning, Donny bopped people on the heads and flipped tassels on his way down the aisle of classmates. Then he strode to the podium, making googly eyes at the audience, who ate it up and laughed with delight. Donny was a good boy, a charming boy. Donny Turn Bull Sherman was definitely *my* boy. My heart burst and my eyes got watery. Oh, how I loved him.

"Well," he said, surveying the front row, "fancy seeing you all here. Come here often, do you?"

Atta boy, Donny! sang my heart as the audience roared with adoration. The fact that Donny was an orphaned former-fatty, the issue of a fourteen-year-old Indian girl and a rapist, the fact that despite such a background, this charming and personable young man was now about to attend Yale—well, it was a success story that made people feel good about themselves and our little school.

"But seriously," said Donny, "I'm very honored to be my class's senior speaker. As many of you may know, I never imagined I'd finish high school let alone be speaking at graduation—as we prepare to go on to colleges and universities and trade schools." And he cocked his head toward Principal Appleton just enough to let everybody know that he was teasing by mimicking the language, and even Appleton laughed.

"I'm grateful and proud to be a member of the class of eighty-eight," he continued. "The world needs us all now more than ever, and I believe our education at Moose Country has prepared us to meet the challenges ahead. I would like to thank Principal Appleton for his vision in creating a school newspaper that has put our little school on the map, giving so many of us opportunities we could never have imagined. Personally, there are so many people to thank for the leg-up I have been given, but I know how anxious we all are to get to the ceremony and the parties!"

Big laugh.

"So I won't bore you with my list. But there is one person that I must acknowledge. A person who personifies the kind of belief and support and generosity every student needs to realize his dreams—"

My heart revved, my sweat glands gushed, my face flushed, and the cold, black hole in my chest suddenly filled with warm stuff. Oh my God, he was going to do it. I dreaded it and I craved it like a lost soul craves a body.

"Without this person, I would not be here today—"

At last!

"Without this person, I would probably be just another Indian high school drop-out—"

If he dragged this out much longer, my deodorized underarm sweat guard pads were going to leak and I was going to have a heart attack.

"Everyone needs someone in his corner, someone who believes in him, a role model, a father figure—"

Huh?

"Mr. Dan Smithson, would you please stand up?" said Donny with the biggest grin I'd ever seen directed at Peggy's father. Embarrassed, Mr. Smithson rose, thumped his chest in a macho gesture of love, pointed at Donny, and then quickly sat down. The audience went wild, clapping and chanting "Smith-son! Smith-son! Smith-son!" until Donny gestured for quiet.

I didn't hear the rest of the speech, and I don't remember the calling of the graduates' names. But finally Mrs. Lambert handed out the last diploma, the children threw their caps in the air, and Principal Appleton yelled, "That's it! You're done!" And carried by the surge of parents and well-wishers, I soon found myself in the adoring crowd surrounding the graduates.

"What a lovely ceremony," said Dorothy Gilhooley, smiling broadly. "You must be so proud of Donny."

"Yes," said I. "So proud."

"Ralph has a small present for him," confided Dorothy, squeezing my arm with excitement. "Do you see him?"

"Right beside you."

"No, silly. Donny. Where is he?" said Dorothy, laughing.

I was too short to see anything, but Ralph raised his hand and pointed. "Over there," he said, pushing through the crowd—dragging Dorothy who was still hanging onto my arm.

"Ever since Ralph's conversion, he's been planning this," said Dorothy, pulling me along. "Making amends, you know. The ninth step."

"Oh," said I.

"Donny! Donny, over here," called Ralph, elbowing people out of his way. "I got something for you, kid." Ralph's face looked like a beet with human features. Tense.

"Oh, hi," said Donny. "Hey, Miss McFigg, didja—"

"Kid, I got you a little gift," said Ralph, planting himself in front of Donny like a road block. "You know, for graduation. It ain't much, but." And he shoved a ring-size box at him.

"Gee, thanks," said Donny, searching for a pocket under his graduation robe.

"Open it now," directed Ralph, refusing to budge.

"Okay," said Donny, and he peeled off the red gift paper and opened a small, white cardboard box. "Gee," he said, struck dumb. "Thanks."

"Put it on," said Ralph, reaching to help.

"No, really, that's okay," said Donny, letting the gold chained crucifix run through his fingers. "Um. This is very nice of you, Mr. Gilhooley. Thanks."

"Call me Ralph, or—Ralph's fine."

"Okay, 'Ralph,'" said Donny uncomfortably.

"Listen, I know you're not Christian, but I wanted to give you something of mine that meant something. Something precious," said Ralph, his eyes imploring Donny for something that neither Donny, nor Dorothy, nor I understood.

"It's very nice, thanks," said Donny, backing away and scanning the crowd for friends.

"I know your mother wasn't Christian, but I don't think she'd mind," said Ralph, his cheeks quivering, his fisted hands shoved down in his pockets.

We were all perplexed.

"Donny," I said, trying to supply a distraction.

"Ralph," said Dorothy.

"You got my eyes!" erupted Ralph. And the world stopped spinning. "*My* eyes. Not your mother's. Now put on the damned chain."

Chapter 26

When Donny left for Yale, he left Moose Country. He called me on holidays, but when I suggested he come for a visit, he always had an excuse. Even Peggy and her famous father-figure father, Mr. Smithson, couldn't entice him to come back.

When Donny left for Yale, he packed everything he owned in his shiny red pickup truck with the engine rebuilt by Ralph Gilhooley. Donny told me he was going to sell the truck as soon as he got resettled, but he never did. That truck got him through four years of college, transporting Templeton wherever he needed to go in return for his assistance in academic matters. That truck moved Peggy from her state school to Cambridge for three years at Harvard Law, then transported himself, Peggy, and Templeton to their three-bedroom New York City apartment on the Upper East Side. Templeton had an entry-level job reporting for a well-known glossy magazine that I will call *Ubiquity*, and Peggy began earning six figures at a Wall Street law firm. Donny had been promised a job at *Ubiquity* too, but he lost it when he failed to show up for his first day and never called. He had recently sold the patent to his grandfather's leverage machine, and apparently the money made him irresponsibly giddy.

But I'm getting ahead of myself.

After Donny left, I remained in Moose Country teaching seventh grade English, directing plays, and overseeing the newspaper. I carefully pulled out of ghostwriting and edited student work, calibrating the quality down just enough to ensure the Sherman legacy. By 1988, there were 5.104 billion people in the world, a first-class postage stamp cost twenty-five cents, "World Music" records with ecstatic drum beats were becoming popular, Prozac was the drug *du jour*, and self-help guru Mr. Tony Robbins said we all had unlimited power and we could achieve whatever we wanted if we just understood that we decide to feel what we feel, and we took the same actions that high-achieving successful people did.

By the summer of 1988, the Montavaldos had ceased coming to their house, but since they wanted to keep it as an investment, they sent me keys and asked if I would mind visiting once a week to check on things if they dropped my rent on the gate cabin by one hundred dollars. I told them I was awfully busy what with my teaching and after-school supervision activities, but I would do my best.

To try to assuage my broken heart over Donny's departure, I decided to add more exercise and structure to my regime. So during the fall of 1989, every afternoon after school, I walked up the long driveway to the Montavaldo house with my *Drums of Passion* record, a yellow legal pad, several black pens, and my tap shoes. For forty-five minutes—per Mr. Tony Robbins—I "decided" to feel exhilarated. I danced, swept away by the syncopated, throbbing, open-hearted music. And when I was done, I collapsed on one of the overstuffed sofas where, having decided to become a famous writer, I took the action of successful writers: I wrote. Slowly I composed on the legal pad. For one month I wrote well-researched stories about rural politics and the educational system, which I then diligently typed and sent out to every appropriate magazine listed in that effete reference for wannabe writers—*Writer's Market*. I explained in my cover letters that I was not a wannabe or a novice, but the experienced and talented faculty editor for the renowned *Moose Country Mutterer*. Nevertheless, my work was largely ignored or rejected by tasteless ignoramuses who responded with pithy pre-printed notes. After I ran out of twenty-five cent stamps, I shifted from journalism to memoir writing because Mr. Robbins said that really successful people weren't stopped by rejection; they just modified their actions according to what they learned from results. Since publishers had no interest in my journalism, I wrote my memoir—until one day I realized that I had no more memoir to tell. I had written my miserable childhood and my even more miserable adolescence—which I suppose, per Mr. Robbins, I decided to feel miserable about. I was a failed thespian who had retreated to the north country where I had been abandoned by the one person I'd ever truly cared about, and now here I was, twenty-eight years old, an interloper in someone else's house—such an insignificant person that I would never even be noticed, even though I had nearly cleaned out the pantry, slowly eating myself to death on nonperishable foods. I hadn't weighed myself since inadvertently stepping on Mrs. Mendelson's scale the day I sprang her bird and burned down her house, and I hadn't been to a doctor since I was thirteen and a half. Yes, I was morbidly obese, but I had no interest in answering questions, or in being naked in front of a stranger, or in taking Prozac, so I didn't see the point. However, I also had no interest in being breathless and dead before my thirtieth birthday, and since Mr. Robbins advised availing yourself of expert help, I burned my memoir and made a phone call.

Don Pedro, the Ecuadorian shaman who'd taught Lurleen Lagerfelt her alternative therapy methods, turned out to be the silver-haired man I'd seen at Grampa Sherman's funeral. I had no interest in therapy, but during my last encounter with Lagerfelt—in the baked goods aisle of the Moose Country Monster Market down at the mall—she had mentioned that her teacher was an herbalist. I didn't know what an herbalist was, but it sounded as if it had to do with food, and Lagerfelt did maintain a lovely figure, so I thought perhaps an herbalist expert could help me with my weight problem.

"Yes," said Don Pedro, looking at me from his doorway.

"How do you do?" said I. And when he didn't answer, "I have a weight problem."

"You are very fat," he said, gesturing for me to come into his house.

The doorway opened into a sunny, plant-filled parlor decorated with earth-toned art that I assumed he had brought from Ecuador. Also, there were a lot of books. This was not what I had expected. Actually, I'm not sure what I'd expected, except, I realized as I looked at the hand-woven orange and brown carpet, the elegant ceramics, and a hand-painted wooden tray full of blue and yellow glass bottles, that I'd presumed Don Pedro was poor. After all, what kind of a living could a shaman herbalist make in a community that, in the space of my life there, had transitioned from hunting and copulating to worrying about their progeny getting into Harvard and enacting zoning laws to forbid visible clothes lines?

"Miss," said Don Pedro, gesturing for me to sit on a spare wooden chair in the center of the carpet. "Please. Thank you."

"Listen, I heard from somebody—I can't say who—that sometimes you crack raw eggs on people. I don't want eggs on this dress."

"Take it off, Miss," he commanded, then shouting to another room, "Brenda!"

In response, the small, fat woman who'd been at the funeral entered. She was almost as fat as I, and I wondered if coming here was a mistake.

As Brenda sat down on the other wooden chair, Don Pedro repeated, "Your dress, Miss," snapping his fingers and turning his back to me.

I don't know if it was his authority, or the presence of the woman, or Don Pedro's complete lack of interest in me, or none of the above, but suddenly his direction seemed reasonable.

"Well?" said I, sitting on the wooden chair in my underwear. "Here's all of me."

When Don Pedro turned back to me, his eyes were closed and he began to hum and whistle. Then he reached out his right hand, and Brenda inserted a bottle into it, signaling that I, too, should close my eyes.

Although this performance struck me as bizarre, I complied, and a few minutes later I felt a light spray all over my back and chest. "Hey!" I said, opening my eyes long enough to see where the spray was coming from. "Hey!" I had put up with a lot of things in my life—from my mother's drinking to Mike the poet's puke to Matilda the drug addict's shooting up. I had been fired and evicted and lost and broke, but never had I been spat on. "Hey!" I repeated, wiping myself and looking for a towel.

"You will clean up later," whispered Brenda. "Allow this."

And against my better judgment, I closed my eyes and tolerated the spit. For ten minutes, the man circled me, singing and whistling and gesturing and beckoning to some invisible something, all the while spitting and spraying me. Finally when he was done, he backed away, gesturing for Brenda to come forward as he left the room.

Thank God that's over, I thought, only to feel Brenda rubbing something that felt like smooth rocks all over my body. Actually, it was rather pleasant—until I took a peek. "Oh no," I said, seeing the eggs.

"Allow," whispered Brenda, gently drawing her hands over my eyelids. "Is good. Allow." And against my better judgment, I closed my eyes as she began to crack the eggs.

When I got home, I took a shower. Then, even though it was early afternoon, I went to bed and slept for fourteen hours. I dreamt about exotic birds in a place with snaky green plants that wound among trees so tall you couldn't see their tops. I dreamt about leopards and lions and alligators that looked like Tony Robbins with teeth the size of rhinoceros tusks. I dreamt I was in the middle of a jungle on the bank of a raging river. I was so hot and the river looked so inviting that I took off my dress. Then I took off my skin, and underneath was another skin—the skin of a beautiful maiden. And suddenly I thought, *What am I afraid of?* And I stepped into the raging river and was swept away.

When I woke, it was three in the morning and I was trembling. I trembled so hard I thought I was going to come apart. My legs and arms, my head, my heart. I trembled with the realization of where I had come from, what I had done, and what I was doing now. I trembled like I *was* the raging river and even though it was scary, it also felt good. So good I was scared. So to make it stop, I ate. Even though I was not hungry, I had a bowl of cereal with banana and strawberries and thick cream instead of milk. Even though I knew from the dream that I was brave enough to be the river, to maybe drop the fat, I ate. And even though I knew Don Pedro had something to do with what I had just learned, I tore up his phone number and threw it in the trash.

And even though it was three o'clock in the morning and pitch black outside, I followed my next impulse and went for a walk. Against my better judgment, I walked for miles, strolling really, and before I knew it, I was standing outside Dorothy and Ralph Gilhooley's house. And even though I knew it was crazy, I decided to go inside and have a look. It was Ralph's fault that Donny had permanently left Moose Country, and I just wanted to see how he lived with himself. Unfortunately, in the throes of curiosity, I had forgotten about the dogs, and that is how Ralph found me, surrounded by a pack of barking canines in the middle of his kitchen at four-thirty in the morning.

Ralph was skeptical, but Dorothy seemed to believe my excuse. She smiled kindly at me and quoted the Bible: "Do not judge or you too will be judged." And then turning to Ralph, "For the same way you judge others, you will be judged, and with the measure you use, it will be measured to you." That seemed to settle it for Ralph because he put down his gun and retreated back to his bedroom.

"Sleep well, Zelda," said Dorothy as she showed me to the door.

And by the end of the week everyone in Moose Country had heard some form of "Bless her heart, Zelda is a sleep-walker."

In a way, it was liberating. Suddenly I had a benign problem that gave me license to explore at my whim.

Chapter 27

During the years that followed Donny's departure, Principal Appleton became enamored with "community building," to use the lingo
du jour. To that end, he scheduled weekly community soirées. Faculty attendance was mandatory, and students and parents were
welcome to come if they liked.

As a skilled reporter, I noticed something about these groups.
When people met in groups, you could see them thinking. With
some people, it was a prolonged thought. With more skillful group
performers, the thoughts might flicker through their eyes at the
speed of a blink, but they were there: "How do I stack up against
the others?" "Am I smarter?" "Is she prettier?" "Do they know my
secrets?"

And when the meetings were over, there were other predictable
behaviors. Some people lingered, chit-chatting, smiling like they
never wondered who was richer or sexier or dumber than they.
Some people raced out, heaving a sigh of relief to escape to solitude.
But there was one thing I'm sure all people had in common. Once
they had returned to their private lives, they would lie on their
couches or watch TVs until they fell asleep. They would eat or

drink too much or fight with their spouses and say nasty things to their children. In some way, they were all secret slobs, doing their best to appear otherwise in the company of others. At least that was my hypothesis when I began my life as an ersatz sleeping-walking burglar. But I was more than willing to learn that I was mistaken.

My second exploratory investigation of the secret lives of others while "sleep-walking" happened several years after visiting the Gilhooleys. Tony Robbins said to find role models, and Dan Smithson was my Donny's father figure, so it felt imperative that I know more.

Peggy Smithson was an only child, and once she had graduated, her parents had no contact with the school. I occasionally spotted Mrs. S in the overpriced organics section of the Moose Country Monster Market. She had a particular interest in the tomatoes, so I lingered over the cucumbers and squash in the adjoining bin long enough to deduce from her conversation with a surgically altered perpetually beautiful transplanted-yuppie mother that the Smithsons were spending the month of October in Mrs. S's parents' country of origin, Sweden—home of the dreaded boarding school that Peggy had avoided by becoming an algebra thief.

I waited until the second week of their holiday, just to be certain. I decided it was best to visit after dusk. Perhaps their lights would be on timers, so I could see, but still be able to make a case for sleep-walking, in the event that I was apprehended. The Smithsons' home was a good three miles from mine, so I drove. After all, if sleep-walking was possible, so was sleep-driving. I drove very slowly, pretending to be in a trance just in case I was being observed by unseen Moosians peeking out through designer blinds.

Designer blinds were all the rage since Blinds & Lampshades by Dahlia had opened—owned by a famous movie star whose real name is not Dahlia. The store was an offshoot of her "get-away house" in Moose Country, where she came to live as "a real person," she told the late-night talk show hosts. She had opened Blinds & Lampshades because she fancied herself a designer, but she had only visited once—on opening day—and left the administration and sales to the niece of the real estate agent who had talked her into the investment. The stuff was fashionably pretentious and came in a lot of pastel colors.

As I parked in a woodsy turn-off about a half-mile from the Smithsons, I filled with excitement: If my hypothesis was wrong, my whole life might change. If there *were* such a thing as genuinely happy and peaceful people, and if the Smithsons were such people, I merely had to copy them to unleash my inner power to do good, lose weight, and become a welcomed and welcoming member of the Moose Country community.

Even though there were no houses between the woodsy turn-off and the Smithsons, I pretended to sleep-walk for the half-mile stroll. When I got to their front door, I paused as if forgetting where I was. Then I knocked several times. Not only was this a brilliant bit of acting, if I do say so, but it was a failsafe measure in case the Smithsons had changed their plans or arranged for a house sitter. Just to be sure the house was empty, I leaned on the doorbell: four ding-dongs and no answer.

Dreamily I strolled around to the back of the house, and when I was sure I was out of sight to any passersby, I took out my set of slim jims and tension wrenches. I'd advanced from my bobby pin after discovering the sweetest little break-in tools in an attractive cowhide pouch in the aforementioned (see prologue) anonymous catalog of hard-to-find and possibly illegal products where I purchased my purse-size antibacterial soaps.

A jiggle, a little push, and I was through the metal door. The screen door wasn't even locked.

As I said, it was just past dusk and the fallen autumn leaves smelled delicious, so I left the main door open to enjoy the breeze. "Honey, I'm home," I called just to make myself laugh. Then I looked around, surprised to be in an office. I knew Mr. Smithson worked at home, but I'd expected to step into a home, not wall-to-wall grey metal file cabinets and a floor littered in lawyer's Redwelds. (I knew the term "Redweld" because back in my New York days, I'd had a small misunderstanding at a law office temp job. Regarding overtime, I believed it should be optional. They did not. So to reimburse myself for emotional distress, I had loaded up on office supplies, including a supply of Redweld expanding file envelopes—one of which miraculously survived Mrs. Mendelson's fire and served as storage for my editorial submissions and rejection letters.)

There was a battered, pock-marked desk with a lopsided swivel chair, an equally distressed sofa with faded, threadbare plaid upholstery. And everywhere there were framed photographs—some custom, some standard in wood, chrome, and blue and red metals. There was Mrs. Smithson smiling under a beach umbrella; Mr. and Mrs. S embracing in front of a brilliantly lit Christmas tree; many portraits of Peggy at all different ages, smiling or mugging for the camera. There was one of Mrs. S holding Peggy as an infant. It almost looked as if she were nursing and Mr. S had snuck up, surprising his wife and catching her response—a nanosecond flirtatious smile infused with naked love for both Peggy and the man behind the camera. It made me blush, but I couldn't stop looking at it. It was in an old wooden frame with a black velvet back, placed in the middle of the desk facing the swivel chair.

Finally, I pulled myself away from it and moved on. The inside door to the office was open and led into a hallway. On the right was a staircase and straight ahead, the living room, dining room, and kitchen. I suddenly felt an urgency to see the whole house so I ignored the impulse to linger over every wall photo. I needed to know the secret.

Which way to go next? I paused at the foot of the staircase and pondered the choice. If you really want to know people's secret truths, you must see where they sleep. I knew this from my own experiences—sleeping in Mike the poet's lumpy chair, then Matilda the drug addict's lumpy futon, my street-found itty-bitty bed in my off-off-Broadway apartment, the concentration camp barracks at the summer theatre, Mrs. Mendelson's bleak furnished room before I burned down her house, and finally in my sweet gate cabin with its two child-size beds pushed together. I tried to remember my bed at my mother's house, but it had evaporated.

Even though the Smithsons' house was empty, I was as quiet as is possible for an approximately two-hundred-thirty-seven-pound lady as I tiptoed up the stairs.

At the top on the right was the master bedroom; on the left, Peggy's room. I went left.

I had forgotten the rumor that Peggy was a horsewoman. She never spoke about it in school, but Donny had inadvertently confirmed it by mentioning that she had a horse boarded at a nearby farm and that she traveled sometimes on the weekends—apparently collecting horseshow ribbons and trophies, which were displayed on the walls of her boudoir. The ribbons made a rainbow on the wall behind her bed of royal blue, red, and yellow—mostly blue, first place of course—which looked rather nice against the robin's egg blue walls with white moldings. The trophies were arranged on a series of stained wood shelves above a stained wooden desk with a neat blotter and sundry supplies placed purposefully around the desktop. I'd heard that Peggy was now living in Cambridge and going to law school. Funny that she'd abandoned all her awards.

The walk-in closet was barren except for a cardboard box full of papers and two cheerleading uniforms, which made me smile. I liked Peggy Smithson. Purposeful and practical. Cheerleading was merely a means to an end: status. The room bespoke a clear, no-nonsense personality who happened to be female. You'd have never guessed she was such a clothes horse. Perhaps because that, too, was a practical means to acceptability in the world. What was most surprising about Peggy's room was that there was really nothing surprising.

I sincerely doubted that there was anything relevant in the cardboard box, but to be a thorough explorer/anthropologist, I thought it best to take a look—several funny birthday cards from classmates, a load of neatly written old homework assignments, and the answers to the seventh grade algebra exams, which made me laugh. Yes, Peggy was a smart one. I was about to replace the papers and move on to the next room, when a piece of monogrammed stationery with uncustomarily sloppy script caught my eye. It was clipped to a copy of my *Moose Country Mutterer* piece about her highly developed fashion sense:

> *How It Is*
> *1. Mom is a witch. I HATE her.*
> *2. I love Daddy, but he wouldn't love me if I told him how much I want to quit horseback riding.*
> *3. Donny loves me a lot. He's cute. I'm not sure I love him back, but maybe it doesn't matter. Maybe somebody loving me—even if it's just for my looks—is the best I'm going to do.*

My word! Perhaps I had underestimated the girl. Not only was she practical, but she was aware and struggling to cope.

Pocketing the paper and the old clipping, I ventured into the master bedroom.

Interestinger and interestinger! Although a man and woman lived here, it was largely feminine with a vanity, two chairs with lacy yellow skirts that matched the yellow Blinds by Dahlia and the pale yellow walls. There was a large antique desk with molded legs and two sets of drawers—his and hers? The bureau, too, looked antique, probably bought at the same estate sale as the rest of the room. The bed had a king-size mattress and an antique backboard. On either side were night tables—one that matched the other furniture, and the other, the only assertion of masculinity in the room. It looked as if a file cabinet and a man's tie rack had merged. It was an odd metal thing with a kind of scaffolding on the top from which hung a gold pocket watch and assorted strings and rubber bands. And on the table were a couple of photographs similar to those in the office. I could almost hear the disputes, but Mr. S had obviously stood his ground.

Had I actually discovered a complicated but happy family, replete with adolescent angst and disagreements over personal styles, who had learned how to cope and compromise? Could this be? To make sure, I decided to investigate the contents of the night tables. Both drawers were locked, but not a problem. In no time, I had jimmied Mrs. S's table and the treasure I discovered made me smile: a diary bursting with paper and letter inserts.

Where to read it? I daren't sit lest my large posterior leave indelible evidence of my visit. I would take it to the master bath. My bladder was excited from my find and I could read while relieving myself.

The master bathroom was spotless with gleaming chrome fixtures and furry pink and tangerine bath towels perfectly folded and hung on white ceramic racks. The white floor tiles looked brand new, so I took off my shoes before entering. The shower curtain matched the towels and was closed. Just to be sure, I peeked behind it, then I laughed at the shock I would have had to discover I was not alone.

I made careful note of everything—the number of folds in the shower curtain, the position of the toilet seat, the placement of the lotions on top of the toilet tank—so I could leave everything as I'd found it. The toilet paper too was folded—like in a hotel—best not to touch, and I checked to see if I had tissues in my purse before sitting. Yes, I had come prepared. I lifted the toilet cover and carefully lowered my bottom onto the seat, shifting until I was comfortable. Then I stared at the diary, simultaneously appalled at what I was about to do and praying that what I was about to do would reveal to me the secrets to happiness that had eluded me for my entire life. I must approach such a tome with reverence. I caressed the worn leather cover as though it were the Holy Grail. I took a deep breath, and exhaling slowly, I opened the book.

It seemed that every page was stuffed with inserted notes, post-cards, odds and ends, and in the front was an envelope full of canceled checks. I'd gone this far, so why hold back? Carefully, I pulled out a paper-clipped bunch of checks with a neatly printed Post-it: "Donny's Tuition." How curious. The checks, signed by both Smithsons, were made out to Donny and on the memo line were little notes: "First Semester. With love, the Smithsons." "Second Semester. The Smithsons believe in you!" etc.

How peculiar. Donny had told me Yale had given him a full scholarship. Who had he lied to? The Smithsons or me?

There seemed to be more inserts than written diary pages, and what was written was rather mundane:

Sunday
  Grocery shopped for the party with the
Powells. Hope the greens stay fresh. Joan is
such a stickler about her salad ever since she
became a vegetarian. What a drag. Note to
self: Make sure Dan's blue shirt is clean for
Monday A.M. meeting.

Thursday
  Dan looked so sweet this morning. He is
such a good husband. How can I?

How can she what? There were a few cards and notes signed "D"
from Dan. Simple reminders mostly:

  Don't forget Donny's check. Due first of
  month.
  —D

And

  I'll bring the wine. Come as you are.
  Love ya, D

Probably a date night reminder. Sweet. Then there was a triple-
folded letter that began, "Darling." As I scanned it for content, my
eye fell to a place mid-way down the page where the handwriting
turned large and emotional:

  I beg you, darling, stop this. Take the anger
  management classes our counselor suggested.

*I know you don't mean what you say when
you get in these spins, but you hurt me
deeply. This simply has to stop.*
      —D

I felt my stomach flip-flop with disappointment and shock. I
wanted to be wrong. I wanted the Smithsons to be as they seemed.
I wanted them to teach me their secrets. I wanted to stop reading
this diary, but I was obsessed. I closed my eyes, flipping pages,
reading where my finger fell.

Wednesday
      *I can't believe we finally did it. Dan had
      taken Peggy to the Northampton Classic, so
      we were alone. I'm so ashamed, but also so
      turned on I'm about to jump out of my skin.
      I'm wicked and I'm evil. But I can't help it.
      I want him. I had him. I want him. It's like
      an addiction. Am I insane? I believe him
      when he says it will stay between us. He is so
      mature and strong. He initiated everything
      and I could not say no. I'm confident he will
      be discreet. But what about me? Oh, Donny,
      Donny, Donny.*

Chapter 28

If you can go into shock from disappointment, I believe that is what happened to me. I stopped caring about much of anything after reading Mrs. Smithson's diary. And oddly, this seemed to make me a better teacher. Nothing riled me—not lateness, dog-eaten homework, or even parents with unreasonable demands, of which there were an increasing number as Moose Country morphed into a Vermont Greenwich with livestock.

Despite my disillusionment about the possibility of true social happiness, I continued to study the increasingly upscale population and I even emulated them on the off chance that accoutrements had some magical happiness-inducing properties. With my reporter's eye, I noticed the dress and accessories of the ladies who attended Appleton's community soirées. And I began to acquire a wardrobe equal to any of the Moose Country yuppie transplants. I had vests to layer with, skirts and dresses of every hem length, sweaters with lace collars, tops with decorative sleeve edges, and shoes to go with every outfit.

In the most respectful and subversive fashion, I educated myself about personal hygiene products: makeup, lotions, and deodorants.

I discovered the secrets of natural-fiber shirts with wicking properties and mouth wash that didn't smell like antiseptic.

And in my effort to become physically acceptable, I also achieved invisibility. I was no longer the extraordinarily fat Zelda or the object of Dorothy Gilhooley's "bless-her-heart" stories. I was simply the English teacher—not a person one would ever suspect of the string of bizarre burglaries that eluded Sheriff Bodwell for more than a decade.

I had not meant to leave the Smithsons' back door open, but as I mentioned, I was in shock from disappointment. Despite my checking and double-checking that everything remained as I'd found it, I seem to have made my final exit through the front door. When the Smithsons returned, Mrs. S insisted on reporting the unlocked back door to Sheriff Bodwell. But apparently Dan Smithson had other ideas. Certain that his wife was being hysterical and had probably left the door ajar herself, he made several behind-her-back winks during the deposition (relayed by the sheriff to Mrs. Bodwell, who told her friend, the new word processing and girls soccer teacher, who of course told Dorothy Gilhooley, and you know the rest), and Sheriff Bodwell, appreciating the male-coded tip, had buried the report in the dead case file.

Emboldened by my success, I plotted future investigatory excursions with a sense of entitlement. Life was not treating me well, and I felt justified in doing whatever was required to discover the secret to happiness.

Despite my improved appearance and diligent use of personal hygiene products, the ladies of Moose Country community soirées did not like me. Oh, they pretended to, but pretense is always detectible: a pinched mouth, a fake smile, over-compensating interested questions. I countered with equal disingenuousness, all the while looking for the truth under our mutual performances: Were they happier than I? If so, why? Were they better in some way? Why did they not accept me and invite me to their homes for dinner? I didn't push or cloy. I was not an hysteric like Mrs. Lambert. What was the secret?

In my quest to solve this conundrum, I selected my burglary subjects by whoever seemed most happy. Mr. Tony Robbins was adamant that the way to success is by modeling successful people. There had to be someone in Moose Country who knew the way to live—a way that once discovered, merely required practice. But over and over I was disappointed. Under every perfect façade were miserable secrets: overwhelming debt, addictions, a transvestite husband and a lesbian wife, bulimia, hoarding, germ phobias, and worse.

I became so disillusioned that some years I didn't bother to burgle. And I believe it was the syncopation of my crimes that allowed me to go undetected. Also, I had so honed my reporter skills as faculty editor of the *Moose Country Mutterer* that I was impeccable in my ability to leave everything as it had been. I was so good that I achieved invisibility as a burglar every bit as complete as what I had achieved as an English teacher. And eventually that led to boredom.

It was in the final year of my hobby that I had the epiphany: what fun it would be to remove one object from a home and place it in the home of my next subjects. It amused me, but also I hoped that if I could ruffle enough perfection, perhaps people would begin to act in public as they were in the privacy of their homes—suspicious, miserable, insecure, longing for that elusive, normal happiness that everybody but they seemed to have. In other words, they would reveal that they were just like me. And I would fit in. It would be incontrovertible.

All went as planned for almost a year. Nobody spoke of their suspicions, but gradually the bizarre stories and accusations piled up at Sheriff Bodwell's office. Neighbors were certain that the people across the street were snooping and entering—either stealing or planting objects in lingerie drawers and kitchen cabinets and medicine chests. This resulted in a thriving new business for Deputy Phil: home security systems—made known to me and every other inhabitant of Moose Country after Deputy Phil got drunk and bragged to Ralph Gilhooley, who told Dorothy, bless her heart.

Foiled by high-tech surveillance and bored with investigative excursions, I returned to my original passion: writing. I rechanneled my creative energy into penning a series of anthropological articles entitled "The Truth about Humans Living Incognito in Rural Northern American Communities," based on my burgling findings (referenced as "fieldwork investigations and interviews" in my bibliography).

I used a pseudonym, of course, and as long as I was at it, I may have added a Ph.D. Several of my articles were published in obscure sociology journals out of Australia, but since I could not claim auteur-ship or cash the checks, after a while the endeavor seemed pointless. To the world I remained an overweight drudge toiling in the trenches of rural lower education—not worthy of being published in, say for instance, that glossy rag, *Ubiquity*, of which Templeton was now the senior editor.

One would think Templeton, of all people, would have been interested in an investigative feature about the secret lives of rural folk—crafted as a generic yet all-encompassing indictment of the burgeoning yuppie colonization of the entire eastern seaboard. In a stroke of inspiration, I reshaped my anthropological articles into an entertaining slice-of-life *divertissement*, written in the voice of a country teacher who was wildly involved in community building and thereby knew all the private, personal details, the hidden decadence, and secret miseries that I had uncovered in my investigative excursions. Although I mailed said *divertissement* in an envelope that was clearly addressed to Templeton, it was summarily rejected by some underling—an over-privileged, minimally educated intern with family connections, no doubt.

To say I was livid is an understatement. I responded to the form rejection with several terribly articulate personal letters to Templeton, and when those did not receive the courtesy of a reply, I wrote to the Letters to the Editor department:

> *Dear Sirs:*
>
> *And I say that advisedly after careful perusal of your masthead which is, I daresay, testosterone heavy in its upper reaches. I have ubiquitously read* Ubiquity *with great interest lo these many years since one of my students began his professional journey there as a cub reporter.*
>
> *Since yours is a publication that espouses truth and social justice, as well as all other liberal causes du jour, I assumed that you would have seriously considered my submissions of late. Or at least have had the decency to explain why you are not interested in publishing timely, original research written in a friendly and accessible tone about the pervasive dishonesty, debauchery, and hypocrisy that are rabidly sphacelating the entrails of the American family.*
>
> *Your artwork and layouts are lovely.*
> *Sincerely,*
> *Z. McFigg*

Needless to say, *Ubiquity* chose not to include my missive in their winter issue.

By my twenty-seventh year educating transplanted yuppie offspring who now had a bloated sense of entitlement encoded into their DNA, I admit I lacked my customary *joie de vivre*. Not only had burgling lost its thrill, but so, too, had the mailing of painstakingly researched stories in the hope of igniting a late-in-life career as a famous authoress. Mr. Robbins's advice to model the actions of successful famous authors that I admired had some holes. Many of my favorites had committed suicide or died drunk and penniless, only becoming famous posthumously, which did not seem like a terribly attractive career path and, quite frankly, it depressed me.

To make matters worse, by the winter of my twenty-seventh year in Vermont, the great recession of 2008 had wiped out much of my hard-earned savings, and the Moose Country faculty's 401(k)s had evaporated in the hands of the infamous investment swindler Bernie Madoff—in whose trust the nouveau-riche president of the PTA had placed our futures.

But to be honest, my malaise was due to something far deeper. I was forty-eight years old and I had lost my faith in the American dream.

Chapter 29

Despite everything, there was one thing I did believe in: the power of a good story told with humor and passion in an authentic original voice. To convey this, I carried on, introducing all of my classes to the works of Mr. O. Henry, Mr. E. B. White, Ms. Sylvia Plath, Mr. John Kennedy Toole, Mr. Jack London, and Ms. Alice Walker.

Several students tried to fake reading Ms. Walker's magnum opus by writing papers based on that cinematic monstrosity starring the most popular talk show hostess in the world, but I set them straight:

"To think that somebody else's interpretation and pictures could be superior to those that you see and hear in your head when you read a great story is idiocy! Are you idiots or students? Now take out your notebooks and write a one-hundred-word essay on the merits of being a student or an idiot—your choice." And this is what I received:

> *At this moment in time of this juncture*
> *where old turns new and books turn obsolete*
> *as the digital age expands to multi-platform*

funky and diverse brands of communication,
to think that reading words on mutilated
tree slices is superior to "la cinema" down-
loaded onto my personal iPhone is idiotic,
not the other way around, Zeldo. IMHO u
suck. And I'm no idiot.

F! If I could have given Walt Edelman a lower grade for this twaddle, I would have, but F is as low as the system would allow. It mattered not that his mother was the president of the PTA who had lost my savings. This was not retribution; it was an honest assessment of the arrogant blather of a student who insulted me with impunity and was committed to destroying twenty-seven years spent considering, developing, and fine-tuning an educational programme. I had lost the American dream; but I would be damned if I'd allow an ignominious scalawag to destroy my curriculum.

In retrospect, I realize that the day Walt Edelman walked into my classroom was the beginning of my undoing. But at the time, I was too blinded by the insult of his smug-faced personage to think strategically about my career goals.

Walt Edelman was shorter than I. A midget. (And I say that with all the derision that little people abhor, since he was not really a dwarf.) He was a stunted being with black nail-polished fingers which he waved to rival Mrs. Lambert in front of band practice. He was a gnome-like thing with over-sized bleached teeth protruding from a flaccid, ever-flapping behemoth mouth. Imagine that over-rated ingénue Julia Roberts's mouth on a four-foot boy with an under-sized cantaloupe head, topped by spiky, over-processed brown hair and tortoise-shell eyeglasses. This is what I had to contend with every day in seventh-grade English class. Is it any wonder I lost control?

Now allow me to set the stage.

Considering my history, I will understand if you are skeptical about my next revelation. But believe me when I tell you that I revered Mr. Walter Cronkite. From the time I was yea big, when I heard his sonorous voice of truth on my inebriated mother's television set, I was smitten. Mr. Cronkite gave me the nightly wherewithal to withstand my mother's spiraling rants against a backdrop of clinking scotch glasses, dripping paint brushes, overturned paint cans, and toxic fumes that, to this day, have affected my olfactory system so that I am never quite sure of the intensity of my stink.

Mr. Cronkite was my role model as faculty editor and ghost journalist for the *Moose Country Mutterer*. If the truth be known, it was Mr. Cronkite's style I copied for my award-winning articles that got Donny accepted into Yale and launched him into a trajectory of successes—most recently as the spokesperson for the new solar-powered filtration systems manufactured by the company that bought Donny's name and Grampa Sherman's leverage machine. The Turn Bull Company had recently received a big chunk of President Obama's stimulus package subsidy money and a contract to supply new infrastructure projects with bio-fuel-powered bulldozers, and it didn't hurt that their spokesperson was a Native American Superman.

But I digress. The point is I worship Mr. Walter Cronkite. He was the closest thing I ever had to a father.

In July of 2009, to pick up some extra money, I had agreed to teach a two-week summer school course called The Basics of Writing. The class was packed due to Moose Country parents' alarm at the propensity of their instant-messaging, texting adolescents to mistake abridged, abbreviated, acronymed vocabulary and butchered syntax for acceptable writing. Sitting in the front row of my first class was Walt Edelman. How I loathed the boy.

"Miss McFugg," he said, mispronouncing by design, "can you please tell us how many and what brand of pencils we should have for this class? My mother will only allow me one number two with a half-eaten eraser. My baby sister likes to chew."

The class roared, and I knew I would have to establish my alpha position now or face the consequences. It was Monday, July 20th. My hero, Mr. Cronkite, had died the previous Friday, and I was not in a jovial mood. "Mr. Edelpuss," I began with no idea what would ensue, "are you so dense or naïve as to think that I would believe the president of the PTA would send her progeny to this esteemed establishment of remedial education with only one half-eaten pencil? Your attempts at creative disruption are matched only by the thimble of grey matter sitting atop your neck that only a loving mother could mistake for a brain."

For the moment of stunned silence that followed I thought I had achieved a victory.

"Miss McFuggle," responded Edelman, his attempted cheerfulness belied by the redness expanding across his normally pasty face, "your ineptitude for teaching a remedial writing course is matched only by your delusions of literacy. *Charlotte's Web* is an old fashioned movie for kindergartners!" He threw up his arms in a victory gesture and the class roared. Then, milking the moment, Edelman rose from his chair, bowed, and parodying my savior, my idol, Mr. Cronkite, he removed his eyeglasses and mimicked, "And that's the way it is."

As the class applauded, I felt something slip loose inside me. Some sliver of a thing that keeps one from strangling contemptible children with flaccid mouths on under-sized cantaloupe heads. I don't know whether it was his disparagement of the work of Mr. E. B. White, or his insult to Mr. Cronkite, or my grief at my loss of the American dream, but before I knew it, I was on Edelman, pushing him into his chair, my fingers closing around his insolent, toothpick neck. I felt his heart pounding as I squeezed and twisted, and I will not lie to you—it was delicious.

And that was the last thing about the incident that I remember. The next I knew, I was lying on the A-frame table, a vestige of the pre-computer days of shop, in Principal Appleton's office, and Mrs. Lambert was jumping and flailing like a crazed band conductor, screaming, "I think she's dead. I never changed her mailbox tag. Oh God, she's dead!"

Chapter 30

I suppose I was lucky to only be stripped of my nonexistent teaching credentials—which paperwork, assigned to Mrs. Lambert, never went through. Ergo, my only punishment for the attempted homicide of a student was to be docked pay and demoted to teaching assistant on the cusp of completing the third decade of my felonious career.

I'm afraid that my change in status—on top of the loss of Mr. Cronkite and the American dream—deepened my already profound malaise to the point that I required medication. And by now you well know my self-medication of choice. To procure said substance, I drove to the mall.

Although it is commonly diagnosed as a disorder, in my opinion, lactose intolerance is only a problem if one lives in the company of others. Since I did not, I intended to pacify my malaise by indulging my love of milk products. I was stocking up on cream cheese, yogurt, and individually wrapped slices of whatever was on sale in the dairy aisle of the Moose Country Monster Market when I ran into the Don Pedros perusing large brown eggs in the organic section. "For your healing rituals?" I queried, assuming they'd remember me, although my herbalist shaman appointment had been many years ago.

"Pedro likes omelets," said Brenda, smiling kindly. She had no idea who I was.

"Ah," said I. "I like eggs too. Scrambled and fried are my favorites."

"You are very fat," said Don Pedro, winking to let me know he remembered.

"Thank you," said I. "I'm flattered that you remember. Unfortunately the healing didn't work. I never lost the weight and I've hit a bit of a rough patch recently. I need comfort foods." And I shamelessly displayed my cartful of creamy delights.

Brenda nodded her many chins, commiserating. Don Pedro turned for the eggs. "Yes, the present is very hard," he said without looking at me. "But you will soon rectify with the past. It is important to notice when the past calls. Travel to it. Good day, Miss. Come, Brenda, it's time to check out. I'm very hungry. You are very fat." And the two of them disappeared down the aisle with his eggs and one tub of imitation butter.

I looked forward to my private evening of binging and flatulence as I drove my VW bug full of milk foods home. I needed an escape. In addition to my professional tumult, life at home had not been restful since the Montavaldos had sold their estate to a new family with three freakishly vociferous young children. Not only had they taken up residence, but for weeks they had been renovating. As I prepared to pull into the canopied gravel nook that was my garage to begin my evening of milk meditation, I was met by a new sign tacked onto my canopy pole, "Tristia House," and a monstrous noise.

"Hey!" yelled a man, running out of my nook and waving his hard hat. "Stop!" Apparently the Tristias had not only decided to name the house, but they were including my nook in their road-paving project; and the men had just poured the tar. "Sorry," yelled another man from atop a truck. And that's when I noticed it was not just any truck. It was a bio-fueled Turn Bull asphalt paver—made by Donny's company. I had been revving up for a fight, but as I remembered Don Pedro's words about the past calling and Tony Robbins's instruction about choice, I swallowed my rage.

"That's okay," said I in my appeasing, non-homicidal former teacher's voice. "I can park right here." And I pretended not to notice the exchange of amused yet disparaging looks as the men watched me struggle out of my car with two bags of carbohydrates.

"You need some help there?" asked the one on foot, making no move toward my car.

"Not at all," I said without looking at him. I had two more bags to fetch and it would be best if I did not establish eye contact. It was bad enough that I could feel their eyeballs tracking me into my house, estimating the size of my behind.

Once I had unloaded all my groceries, I locked my door, closed my pale yellow designer blinds, and turned on a CD loud enough to drown the noise of the machinery. "I'm a fool to want you," sang Mr. Sinatra, "Pity me, I need you"—I could still hear the men's sarcastic remarks. "I know it's wrong, it must be wrong," sang Sinatra several decibels louder as I pressed volume on my remote. "But right or wrong, I can't get along without you."

Several hours later, just as I was preparing to sit down with a plate of chips and a bowl of chocolate, vanilla, and mint chocolate ice cream to consider my career goals as a teaching assistant, there came a knock on my door. I was not about to let those rednecks see me eating. "Just a minute," I called, hurriedly hiding my feast behind the television set. It was almost dusk, and I was in Matilda the drug addict's grandmother's slightly smoke-damaged nightie. If they asked me to move my car, screw Tony Robbins, I would tell them to go to hell. "Yes?" I said, opening the door just enough to see that it was not the men. "Oh, hello," I said, surprised.

"I'm so sorry to bother you," said Mrs. Tristia, a twenty-five-year-old who had married into enough money to renovate the Montavaldo estate, maintain apartments in New York and Paris, and never worry about career goals. "I tried to call you earlier, but you don't have an answering machine."

There was an awkward silence as she waited for me to open the door and invite her in. "I was out," I replied in my implacable teacher's voice. "What can I do for you?"

"Well," said Mrs. Tristia, debating whether to request entry.

"I'd ask you in, but I'm afraid I was just about to step into my bath," said I.

"Well," said Mrs. Tristia, looking this way and that, trying to peek through my cracked door. She had only seen the inside of my gate cabin once—just before the house closing—as the Montavaldos, unlike me, were respectful of privacy.

"Perhaps you would like to call me on the telephone tomorrow," I suggested. If she kept me much longer, my feast would melt, overflowing onto my new combination VCR/DVD player. "I shall be up and about by nine."

"Actually," said Mrs. Tristia, "I wanted to do this in person."

Oh God.

"As you know," she continued, "we love the house and the grounds. And I want you to know we'll give you all the time you

need to find a new home..." And the rest was like someone bab-
bling under water.

I don't know what time it was when the phone rang. Midnight, one,
two A.M.? All I know is that ever since the landlady's visit, I'd been
eating and farting with abandon. When I answered, I was in a milk
products-induced stupor, so at first I didn't recognize the voice.

"Hey," he said.

"Who is this?" I demanded, certain that it was Edelman playing
a prank to suffuse my gaping wounds with salt.

"Me," he answered.

"Who?" I repeated. The logy, maybe drunken voice was vaguely
familiar.

"It's me, Zelda," said forty-two-year-old Donny. "Please don't
hang up."

Chapter 31

It was August 2009 when Donny called, and a week earlier Mr. Ted Kennedy had died. After Mr. Cronkite, Mr. Kennedy was my next choice for a father. I know he did bad things, but the fact that he stopped made him my second choice. So please try to understand the depth of my despair: Mr. Kennedy was dead, I had been demoted, evicted, and I was sitting in a chamber of my own gaseous emissions in a lactose stupor when Donny called after more than two decades without communication. He called to tell me he was distraught because Peggy had left him. It had been a big misunderstanding, he said, sounding sloshed.

"What happened?" said I.

"She walked in on me in bed with Carla Dusenbacher."

Donny had the most endearing laugh and his ridiculousness made me miss him. "Who's Carla Dusenbacher?" I wanted to know.

To make a very long story a little less long, here's what happened: As I mentioned, Donny was the indigenous spokesman for the Turn Bull Machinery Company, and as such had appeared on the *Today Show*. His assignment had been to represent one of the newly "greened" companies receiving stimulus money as part of the Obama administration's recession recovery program. But in a fit of competitive ardor with the other green panelists, Donny had suddenly announced a nonexistent Turn Bull Young Activists Initiative. The executives at Turn Bull were furious…until a producer from the world's most popular talk show—which I will now refer to as the *Olga Show*—called. The producer, Carla Dusenbacher, said Miss Olga herself had been intrigued with his *Today Show* appearance, and Carla wanted to meet with Donny to discuss a joint venture. One thing led to another, and then Peggy walked in.

Donny and Peggy had never married. Donny had asked, but Peggy, with her lawyer's intuition and keen sense of good strategy, had refused. After she caught Donny with Carla, she gave him the apartment and moved to a new luxury high-rise in Tribeca.

Weepily, Donny told me that next month he was scheduled to appear on the *Olga Show* to announce a joint venture between Turn Bull and the Olga Corporation—complete with a new magazine for young activists to be called O^2. Donny was to be editor-in-chief due to his bogus journalism background and Yale education, but he didn't know if he could go on without Peggy.

In Donny's defense, I never told him that I had been evicted and had decided to quit my job at the height of the recession. I didn't tell him I assumed there would be a job for me at O^2. I never said that since I had written every word he had ever taken credit for, I believed some sort of compensation was due now that I was forty-eight years old, unemployed, and homeless.

Although I don't believe in psychics, Don Pedro's words about rectifying the past and traveling to it had given me the confidence that I was doing the right thing when I packed my possessions into

Grampa Sherman's VW bug and drove to the Upper East Side of Manhattan to begin anew as Donny's peer. At age forty-two, Donny was no longer my student. He was newly single, and I was too old to remain a virgin.

My plan was to help Donny in an honest, collegial, mutually beneficial way. I would build the infrastructure of O^2 as I had for the *Moose Country Mutterer*. I would write a mission statement, create the editorial voice, assign articles, and edit same. In return, I expected a salary and a title on the upper reaches of the masthead—rectification of the past.

"Zelda!" said Donny when I arrived at his apartment at six P.M. with two suitcases, a duffle bag, and my Redweld of articles and rejection letters. "What are you doing here?"

"You invited me," I responded. I didn't know which was more stunning, his surprise or his appearance. My boy had turned into a glorious, albeit haggard, man with salt and pepper hair, a five o'clock shadow, and the same self-deprecating smile I remembered—and it still turned my heart to mush. "You called me. Don't you remember?"

"Of course, of course," said Donny. "I'm sorry, come in."

I could smell the booze on his breath, but this was not a problem. We had solved this issue before. "The drive was horrendous, but your doorman was extraordinarily helpful," I said, dragging my duffle bag behind me.

"Oh God, I'm an idiot," said Donny, grabbing it out of my hand. "Come in, come in."

"I never could have gotten myself into the elevator without his upper body strength," said I, admiring Donny's. "I only had a fifty, so I didn't tip him. Perhaps you could take care of that later. Nice place—you even have security officers. They asked me to tell you not to forget your package. So...where am I going to sleep?"

Donny looked confused, and I wondered if he remembered any of our conversation. Not a problem. He was obviously in desperate need of my assistance, and all would be well as soon as we discussed a plan.

"I guess you have a choice," said Donny, suddenly looking limp. "Peggy always used that room as her office, but it has a pull-out couch. And after Templeton moved, we turned the other one into a guest room. Peggy did it. I haven't touched anything."

Donny's apartment was way more spacious and airy than Mike the poet's, Matilda the drug addict's, or my own teensy off-off-Broadway hovel a lifetime ago. The living room was twice the size of my gate cabin with IKEA-type furniture, which, considering Peggy's Scandinavian roots, made sense. The walls—robin's egg blue with white moldings—were reminiscent of Peggy's bedroom and, had Donny not been living alone for two weeks, I could imagine this place would have been a pleasant and attractive domicile. I made a mental note of the crushed beer can and empty whiskey bottle trail through the dining room alcove and into the kitchen, and I wondered if this might be a bigger project than I had anticipated. Donny had mentioned on the phone that he was having trouble with the O^2 outline and the evidence of that was underfoot.

I kicked crumpled paper balls out of my way as I opened the door to the guest room. There were the yellow designer blinds I remembered from Mr. and Mrs. Smithson's room and a single bed with a pastel quilt. There was a small blonde wood bureau with white enameled knobs decorated with hand-painted teddy bear faces, and a butterfly mural peeked out from the wall above the toilet in the guest bathroom.

"Peggy originally thought this would be a nursery," said Donny, heaving my bags onto the travel rack. "We never got around to redecorating. You hungry, Zelda?" But before I could answer he slurred, "Help yourself to whatever you want in the kitchen. I'm afraid I forgot to shop. Hey, listen, it's great to see you, but the truth is I'm a little drunk so how's about we say our real hellos in the morning? Sleep tight, Zelda." And he was gone.

I am not a stupid woman. I knew Donny was a mess. I knew he had alcohol, sex, and possibly several other addictions. I knew he had lost his soul and sold his name and was capable of elaborate deceptions. But so had I addictions. So was I lost. So did I deceive and manipulate. So who better to rescue Donny than I? It was never too late to change your ways. After all, Mr. Ted Kennedy, once a womanizing drunk who had abandoned a lady to her death in a drowning car, had turned into the patriarch of an extended family of fatherless children as well as the preeminent spokesperson and legislator for the most helpless and hopeless of our species. It is *never* too late to change. So said Tony Robbins. So said I to myself as I drew back the pastel quilt, switched off the merry-go-round nightstand lamp from Dahlia's Designer Blinds & Lampshades, and once again climbed into a child's bed to sleep.

Chapter 32

Perhaps it was being back in New York. As in the old days with Mike the poet, the next morning I woke at dawn, silently did my morning ablutions, tidied the apartment, and borrowed Donny's house keys on my way out to procure a nutritious breakfast.

I do love New York in the morning. I walked without being bumped, and now that I no longer hated people, I could relax. From the outside, the vegetable and fruit markets looked the same as I remembered, but inside was a different world: spotless chrome deli bins piled with steaming scrambled eggs, home fries, and assorted fruit mixes. There was bubbling oatmeal, pancakes that smelled like cinnamon, and crispy brown waffles. And above the bins was a neat line of miniature cold cereal boxes and pitchers of milk and juices.

I wasn't sure what Donny liked, so I bought a little of everything as well a pot-load of fresh, black coffee for his inevitable hangover. I loaded up on napkins, and for old time's sake, I bought several packages of peanut butter and cheese sandwich crackers. The fresh-faced Puerto Rican cashier smiled sweetly as she rang up my purchases, put the coffees in plastic, and carefully loaded my entire order into two large, recycled paper shopping bags. "Have a nice day," she said as she handed me change from my fifty.

The idea that my Donny was turning into a drunkard was untenable, and I could not wait to feed him and discuss our future professional collaboration as true equals.

My stomach was making a terrible noise as I stepped into the elevator. The doorman once again assisted me with my packages, and I felt bad that my hands were too full to tip him.

"Please tell Mr. Donny he has a package at security," he said with an expectant smile.

"Sure thing," said I. I would return with a fresh ten dollar bill immediately after breakfast.

When I got to the sixteenth floor, I quietly let myself in, calling, "Donny, it's Zelda," so as not to startle him.

To my surprise, Donny was dressed, shaved, and sitting at the dining table reading the *New York Times*. "Hi," he said cheerfully. "Thanks for cleaning up. I'm sorry I was so out of it last night. I know you have a thing about alcohol because of your mother. I'm really not a drunk, Zelda. It's just Peggy, you know?" And he looked so forlorn it was all I could do not to hug him.

"I brought breakfast," I replied. "And the doorman said you have a package at security."

"You're wonderful," he said, brushing aside the newspaper. "Let's have breakfast here."

"Also coffee," I said, pulling out the plastic bag. "Strong."

"Zelda, Zelda, Zelda," he almost chanted, "what would I do without you?" And he pulled out the first Styrofoam cup, poured it into his empty mug, and took a long drink. "Olga wants a complete outline of O^2 by next Tuesday," he said, leaning back in his chair and letting the caffeine do its work.

And even though I knew we had a monstrous job ahead of us, I was so filled with love and confidence about our future that I merely laughed and said, "Zelda's here. No worries."

Since Donny had said that O^2 was meant to inspire young people, I drew on my nearly three decades of teaching and suggested we first inspire them to read the magazine by opening with an easy-to-read story. "It could be a profile of a young person who has made a difference in somebody's life—sort of like the young guests Olga likes to showcase. You know, the cripples and people who have been sexually molested but are now sharing their stories of heartbreak and tragedy in order to simultaneously give their suffering purpose and save others from similar catastrophes."

"I don't know," said Donny.

"We need a cute title."

Donny drained his coffee cup and thought hard.

"How about 'Making a Difference'? The personal tragedies will just be a side benefit. Sort of like that new TV talent show where the contestants who were once paraplegic tell about how they had to relearn walking and eating before blowing everybody away with their singing and dancing routines. The tragedy is subliminal to make you feel all warm and fuzzy."

"If you say so," said Donny. "Write it down."

It was two o'clock and Donny hadn't budged from the dining table where we had started the meeting. He had his laptop open, even though we'd decided, for this stage of the outline, it would best if I relax on the couch and scribble on a yellow legal pad. Donny had a pad as well. So far, he had read the *New York Times*, paged through his laptop "favorites," and made a doodle of me scribbling notes for the whole front of the magazine:

O² Outline
1. _Table of Contents_
2. _Letter from Donny_
3. _Letters to the Editor_
4. _Coming Attractions_
5. _Column: "Making a Difference"—profile
of a young activist who has overcome severe
obstacles to become an asset to society and a
hero to those in need_

"Okay, what's next?" said I, after finishing the description blurb. "Do you have any magazines we could look at?"

"Just _Ubiquity_. Boy, Templeton really found his niche. What a racket, huh?"

I wasn't sure what he meant, so I just said, "Hmm," and accepted the issue he pulled out from under his _New York Times_. "We need a section of news tips, then features," said I, after flipping through half a magazine of advertisements. "For that, we need writers... unless you intend to—"

"Get real," said Donny laughing.

I laughed too. At least we both acknowledged the truth. "So how do we find writers?" said I, suddenly realizing I was not in Moose Country anymore.

"Beats me," said Donny, laying his head on his arms on the dining table the way he used to do in study hall.

"I suppose there's a way to use the Internet," said I, closing _Ubiquity_.

And then as if sharing one mind, we both said it: "Templeton!"

Donny made the call and I made my private peace. I would not mention my rejected submissions and unacknowledged letters when Templeton came for an evening of friendly brainstorming and pizza. I cleaned up the breakfast dishes and completely forgot about tipping the doorman.

Chapter 33

Templeton's metamorphosis surprised me even more than Donny's had. What had once been a wiry, under-developed boy body had turned into a powerful, solidly muscled man. Despite his short stature, Templeton had the lanky, graceful appearance of a marathon runner. His hair was still brown and pulled back into an intellectual's ponytail. And he'd exchanged his bulky plastic glasses for the rimless lenses made popular by the idiot savant from Alaska who had briefly run on the Republican ticket for vice president. (And please do not assume you know my political affiliation from this or earlier comments. I assure you I am an equal opportunity disparager—otherwise known as unaffiliated.)

"Miss McFigg," said Templeton with a touch of irony.

"Please call me Zelda," said I. "It's been a long time. Won't you come in? Donny's getting the pizza and will be back in a minute."

"Well, well, well," said Templeton, strolling past me into the apartment. "Haven't seen this place since the day those two kicked me out."

"Ah," I answered because it seemed most diplomatic. Donny had neglected to tell me this story, but I got all the details from Templeton's comment. "Well, isn't it time to let bygones be bygones? After all, you've done pretty well since then."

"Water under the bridge," said Templeton, plopping down on the couch. "So how's things with you, Zelda? Still torturing the kids with *Charlotte's Web*?"

I blushed and swallowed. We needed Templeton's expertise, so, per Tony Robbins, I would monitor my thoughts, choose my emotions, control my responses, and not allow myself to be upset by puerile put-downs. "I'm afraid I'm no longer teaching. The recession, you know. Cut-backs."

"I'm sorry to hear that," said Templeton with complete disinterest as he spied a copy of *Ubiquity* on the coffee table under his feet. "I didn't know he still subscribed."

"Donny has always supported you," said I, because it sounded relationship-enhancing.

"You don't say?" said Templeton, picking up the magazine. "You like our covers, Zelda?"

"I think they're very attractive. Can I get you something to drink? Donny should be here any second."

"Scotch," said Templeton, and blessedly the door opened and Donny entered with an armload of pizzas and three bottles of scotch whiskey.

"Sorry I took so long. There was a line. Hey, Templeton, howzit going? Long time, no see. No, don't get up. I'll put it all on the table."

"Hey, asshole," said Templeton, making no move to get up.

"He means that in the most complimentary way," said Donny, shooting me a smile. "Listen, Templeton, I really appreciate your coming. Zelda and I are ignoramuses when it comes to the new fangled cyber world."

"Whatever," said Templeton, resisting flattery. "So how's Peggy? Working late as usual?"

"She left me, man," said Donny. "What are you drinking?"

"Scotch on the rocks," said Templeton, a gleeful smile twitching on the corners of his mouth. "Sorry to hear that, man. That's a real shame."

Templeton talked. I took notes on my yellow legal pad. And Donny drank.

Templeton told us about journalists' associations, freelance unions, and writers' group web sites. He gave us URLs for listserves where people asked for sources and story experts and others where writers looked for assignments. He told us about twaddling and bulging and social nattering and all manner of Internet information sharing. And not once did Donny ask a question.

"Let me ask you a question," said Templeton after an hour and a half.

"Sure," said Donny. "Anything."

"Who's running this rag, you or Zelda? The reason I ask is, although we go way back, I think it's only fair that I get something for my input. Maybe a consulting editor credit and some kind of honorarium. How about we put something in writing?"

Donny sipped scotch. Templeton watched him, his beady rat eyes dancing behind his rimless lenses. I watched Templeton watching Donny. It had never even occurred to me to ask for a contract before quitting my job and driving ten hours in an antique VW bug. This was very interesting; *watch and learn*, said a little voice in the back of my head. *The rat is smart.*

"The Olga Corporation is in charge of all that stuff," said Donny finally. Then recovering his smile, "Write something up—whatever you think is fair—and I'll pass it on to Carla Dusenbacher, Olga's producer. She likes me. I'm sure it'll be okay."

I noticed he never answered the question about who was running this rag. Templeton glanced at me, then looked at the floor. He knew—about now and high school. He knew it all. The rat was smart.

"Take care of yourself, Zelda," he said a little later after Donny had excused himself.

"I certainly intend to," said I, showing him to the door. "You have been most helpful."

If we were to have a fully-fleshed-out proposal for O^2 by Tuesday, we needed a list of sample short articles and features. Donny was passed out in his room, so that night I wrote the "Call for Submissions" myself:

> *Young Activists and Writers: Contribute your story ideas for a new magazine about making a difference—to be published by a mega-media giant in entertainment. No payment now, but future employment if we use your stories.*

As Templeton had suggested, I registered for a free email account and used that address for contact. Then I posted the blurb on three of the top writers' web sites on my yellow legal pad. And just out of curiosity I took a look at the other help-wanted listings. They all appeared to be some version of:

> *Wanted: Energetic social-nattering genius who's an aggressive multi-tasker, driven to multi-task at multi-levels with aggression and drive, proficient in PhotoFake, XYZ and LMNOP softwares, obsessive about details and deadlines—to work in a fast-paced, exciting, multi-platform marketing, PR, and aggression-driven new agency. Massive overtime evenings and weekends expected. Salary lo 40s.*

I turned off Donny's computer. Tomorrow I would insist on a masthead title and a contract.

Chapter 34

There were seven hundred twelve email submissions for *O²* the next morning. Some were idea pitches and others were full-fledged stories. "Oh my God," I said to Donny over our pot of deli coffee. "How are we going to sort through these?"

"I have complete confidence in your editor's eye and administrative genius," said Donny, rubbing sleep out of one eye and turning the page of his *New York Times*. "We both know you're awesome."

I knew I had to broach the subject of my position and salary, but perhaps it would be best to wait until he'd recovered from his hangover and finished reading the *Times*.

For the entire morning and a good part of the afternoon, I read and sorted queries, rejecting most and finally resorting to form letters *sans* explanations. And I made a mental note to be nicer to Templeton the next time I saw him. If my measly ad attracted seven hundred twelve responses overnight, I could only imagine what *Ubiquity* received in their daily mail.

At three o'clock the phone rang and I had my chance to make amends for years of resentment. "Hello, Templeton," I said, feeling the first real compassion I'd ever felt for the boy-turned-man. "We really appreciated your input last night. I did what you—"

"Let me talk to Donny," he interrupted.

"I'm afraid he's not here," I said, determined to maintain my good feeling. "He went out for—"

"Okay, I don't care," snapped Templeton. "Could you just tell me his fax number?"

"Fax?"

"It's in Peggy's office. I saw it when I was looking for the bathroom."

I'd noticed Templeton snooping, with the pretense of not knowing there was a bathroom off the dining room of the apartment he'd lived in for two years. "Hold on, I'll go look," said I, knowing that of the two of us, I was far guiltier in the snooping department.

After I'd given him the number, Templeton coughed. Then he said, "Will you tell Donny I'm faxing a consulting editor agreement? And, by the way, if my name's going to be on this rag, we need another meeting so I can make sure it doesn't suck. I'll be there at six o'clock. Also, I left a voice mail for Peggy at her job. We need a lawyer to sit in. If she can't make it, I'll bring somebody from *Ubiquity*. And can you please get some pizza without olives this time?" Click.

My, it was hard to stay cordial, but I did forgive Templeton for ignoring my submissions.

Despite a feeling of weight that had nothing to do with my bulk, I prepared for the evening's meeting. I typed and printed four copies of a complete O^2 breakdown by department, and within the departments, potential stories, story topics, along with possible writers with brief bios. Brought to their knees by the recession, a host of well-

known journalists and book writers had responded to my Call for
Submissions, so I was able to create an impressive list of prospective
contributors. I made an editorial calendar of features, adding my
own ideas to fill things out. And at the bottom of each printed breakdown, I signed my name. I figured if all these credentialed people
were willing to work without even knowing the salary or the name of
the publisher, I'd better ensure my own position by signing my work.

Donny didn't get home until five forty-five, so I barely had a
chance to tell him about the meeting before the doorman buzzed
to say Templeton was here and he'd brought Miss Peggy. "Just
calling to let you know. They're on their way up. I gave Miss Peggy
your package."

"Thanks, George," said Donny. At the mention of Peggy's name
his haggard look evaporated and a dopy expression came over his
face. "Peggy's back," he whispered to the heavens, and he ran to
open the door.

As it turned out, nobody was interested in my breakdowns and
editorial calendar. Templeton glanced at both and said they looked
good to go, then Peggy and Templeton started pelting Donny with
legal questions:

Who owned what rights?

What salary guarantee was there for Templeton? (He handed
Donny his contract because, it turned out, the fax had been
disconnected.)

What were titles and masthead positions?

How much did Donny stand to make on this deal, and what
percentage might be due Peggy in recompense for her contribu-

tion to his support over the lean years? She said she would take a percentage in lieu of a fee for her legal services when she reviewed everyone's contract.

"Everyone's contract." That made me perk up. "Everyone" included me. Thank God for Peggy Smithson. She would take care of me, and I'd never have to confront my boy Donny with unpleasant business matters.

"So how've you been, Zelda?" said Peggy after the meeting broke up.

"Call me Zelda," I said jokingly. She caught my eye and we both laughed. I had always admired Peggy. And now, even more so. She had matured well. Still tall, blonde, and fashionable, but she had a tired expression as well as the old sadness behind those beautiful turquoise eyes, and it gave her another dimension. Wisdom? I wondered if she'd ever found out about her mother and Donny. I wondered if she'd ever told her father she didn't like horseback riding. I wondered how many miscarriages or how many of Donny's affairs—sensed but not discovered—had led to her decision to give up on the nursery. "I'm just fine," I answered. "How about you? Are you still collecting blue ribbons?"

Peggy looked startled, and to cover the source of my knowledge, I blurted, "Donny once mentioned your competitions—back when you were in high school."

"Oh," said Peggy. "No, I don't do that anymore. It was really my father's interest more than mine. I just did it to make him happy." Then she looked at me hard. "Zelda," she said, her eyebrows furrowing and unfurrowing.

"Yes?" said I.

"Nothing really," she answered after a thought. She took a few steps toward the door. "Take care of yourself, Zelda," she said, turning back to me. And that's when I saw the look. It was not wisdom. It was pity—focused on me.

"Take care of your own self," said I, opening the door. And she walked out.

I don't know which is worse, being mocked or pitied, but pity feels worse to me.

In his excitement at seeing Peggy, Donny had limited his alcohol intake to three scotches—which, because of his size, made no difference in his demeanor. At least he appeared sober to me. He was jovial and helpful with the kitchen clean-up, and I began to feel warm again.

"Do you think I'm pathetic?" I asked, catching my reflection in the pot I was washing.

"Hell, no," said Donny, giving me a goofy look. "Where'd that come from? You are the least pathetic person I've ever known, Zelda. Hell, if anyone's pathetic, it's me. I thought Peggy might come back. What a jerk I am." And with a suddenness that took my breath away, he sank to the floor with his face in his hands and cried. He cried like a broken old man, and it was all I could do to hold him.

"Oh, Donny. Oh my Donny," I cooed, rocking him against my bosom. And Donny curled up as much as a six-foot-three-inch man can in the lap of a four-foot-eleven-inch morbidly obese lady, and we sat there until he was cried out.

I don't know how much time went by, but eventually, without speaking, Donny stood up and offered me his hand—which I took. Then we walked together into his bedroom.

We both got undressed, and I wasn't embarrassed. We lay there. We lay in each other's arms and didn't make love—although, had he been willing, I might not have said no.

"Donny," I said many hours later. He groaned and I was not surprised that he'd instantly responded. "Donny," I said, "what about my position at O^2? I'm almost fifty years old and I need a job. I quit Moose Country and moved out of my house."

There was no answer for a long time. Then, rolling onto his side away from me, Donny mumbled—just like the old days—"Don't worry about it, Zelda. I'll take care of it."

Chapter 35

Templeton was furious. "Sherman, you have screwed with me for the last time!" he yelled—so loud that I could hear him through Donny's phone receiver. Donny held the receiver tight against his ear and was turned away from me. The screaming continued for several minutes, and when it stopped, Donny mumbled something I couldn't make out and hung up.

"What was that about?" I said, clearing our pizza plates—Donny had left a full inch of crust. "He sounded pretty angry. I could hear him from the kitchen."

Donny shrugged and shot me his goofy smile. It was a week since our night together, and although neither of us had spoken of it, we both felt a new intimacy. Or at least I did.

"No really, I want to know what he said," I insisted, feeling a new and delicious sense of entitlement and wondering if Donny would notice if I ate his leftovers.

"It's not a big deal. He's just being a pain in the butt. Olga wants some changes in his contract. It's cosmetics. He'll still get his damned money. The guy's a glorified rewriter, but you know Templeton."

I choked on the crust I'd just nibbled. I had to stop eating other people's leftovers. "So Olga has gone over the contracts?"

"I guess," said Donny, padding into the kitchen.

I stopped cleaning and took a breath. If I didn't assert myself now, Peggy was right and I was pitiful. "What about me?" I said as Donny reappeared with a new beer. "I'm not just a glorified rewriter...anymore."

"What *about* you?" said Donny, looking puzzled and ignoring my last comment.

"My contract, my salary, my position at the magazine. Did she say anything?"

"Did you give me a contract?" asked Donny, cracking open the beer and tossing the aluminum tab on the table.

"No," I answered. "You said you'd take care of it."

"I did?" said Donny.

"Yes, you did," said I.

Donny shrugged and padded into the living room with the remote and the unopened package that had been sitting on the sideboard since Peggy's visit. "Then I guess I must have done it."

Oh how I wanted to let this go and trust that my boy Donny would take care of me. "You don't remember doing it?" said I, following him into the living room.

"Not really. But that doesn't mean anything. I do lots of things I don't remember." And he laughed in that self-deprecating way that was usually contagious. "Like this package. I can't even remember what I ordered." And he began to unwrap it.

"I need to know if you've spoken to Olga or Carla Dusenbacher or anyone at the Olga Company about a commitment to me, Donny."

"God, Zelda, you're starting to sound like Templeton. Will you give it a rest? If I said I'd do it, I'm sure it's done. Carla is a very busy person. I don't want to bug her. Trust me. I'm good at this kind of negotiation. Hey, how about some popcorn?"

I love popcorn, but suddenly I had a freakish lack of appetite. "What title did you ask for for me?"

"Title schmitle. Carla will work all that out. Oh God," he said staring into his package and blushing. "Personal stuff." And he quickly resealed the box. "So what were you saying?"

"I think managing editor, under your name on the masthead, would be fair. I planned the whole issue, which is more than Templeton did."

"Hey, speaking of that," said Donny, smiling broadly and opening his arms for an air hug, "did I tell you? Olga loved your front-of-the-book column about kids?"

"No, you didn't tell me," said I. I not only lacked appetite, but an intense nausea was spreading through my upper tract.

"She just wants one little change," said Donny, turning back to the TV and channel surfing on his remote "She wants to call it 'Olga's Kids' and take the byline. She won't actually write it, but her staff will pick the crippled or underprivileged kid each issue and somebody on staff will ghost-write the profile."

"So you *are* discussing staff," said I.

"Not really," said Donny. "Carla will take care of all that. I think she has a crush on me."

And I realized he'd completely forgotten that he'd told me he'd slept with her. What the hell—*who* the hell's hands was I trusting to take care of me? "And when is Carla going to hire staff?" said I, breathing steadily to keep my voice from shaking. I don't know why, because Donny seemed unfazed, immersed in a choice between *Survivor* and a game show.

"As soon as she gets an okay on the budget," said Donny happily. "Olga wants a lot of big names, and Carla knows everybody.

I think she has the hots for me, but don't worry, I'm keeping this strictly business."

"Donny," I said as calmly as I could, "I need to ask a question about a whole other topic. Do you mind if I change the subject?"

"Please," said Donny, deciding to watch *Survivor*. "God, I love this show."

"It's about when you went to Yale. I seem to recall that you told me they gave you a full scholarship."

"Yup," said Donny. "Why do you ask?"

"So you didn't have to pay for anything?"

"Nope. Not even books. I got a stipend."

"Are you sure, Donny?" And something in my voice made him finally turn away from the TV.

"Of course I'm sure. I was the sole beneficiary of the Yale Endowment for Early-admitted Native Americans—Yee-Na! or 'What a lot of wampum,' as we NA's like to say. Some rich, guilty white guy left earmarked funds, and I was the only Indian who applied my year. What's all this about, Zelda?"

"Nothing," said I. "Forget I asked."

Two days earlier I had received a letter forwarded by the Moose Country Post Office. It was from the Montavaldos:

> *Dear Zelda,*
> *We hope this letter finds you. The new own-*
> *ers didn't have a forwarding address, but we*
> *trust you left instructions with the post office*
> *and we understand you've moved back to*

*Manhattan. We will certainly understand
if this is not convenient, but we have a favor
to ask. Mr. Montavaldo has been suddenly
transferred to Italy and we've left our affairs
in a little disarray. Our Fifth Avenue apartment will be empty for three months, except
for weekly visits from the housekeeper, and
we wonder if you would mind checking
in. . .*

Since they said it would be fine if I stayed in the guest room until
the subletters arrived, I quietly packed my bags.

"Donny," I said when I was done.

"Sure," said Donny, engrossed in a show about psychopathic
housemates.

"I'm moving to the Montavaldos' apartment. I'm leaving the
phone number here under your scotch bottle. Please call when you
hear about my contract."

"Sure thing," said Donny, draining his sixth beer.

"And thanks for letting me stay here."

"No prob," said Donny. "What a jerk! I'da seen that coming.
Everybody on these shows is so stupid."

"No need to get up," I said, and I let myself out.

Chapter 36

It was even harder loading my two suitcases, duffle bag, and Redweld file into the elevator going down than it had been coming up. And when I got to the lobby, George the doorman, was very slow to help me.

"Sorry, Miss, I've got to stay at my station," he said after dumping my bags on the sidewalk in front of the building. And that's when I discovered that my car had been stolen.

"You mean you didn't notice anyone breaking in?" I asked, incredulous.

"Sorry, Miss," said George, with a helpless shrug. "Things happen fast around here. I must've been on a break."

I hailed a taxi.

I don't remember the ride to Fifth Avenue, and I don't remember who helped me out of the taxi or the conversation about my staying in the Montavaldos' penthouse. I barely remember moving in or exploring, if I did explore. I had lost my taste for snooping. The next thing I do remember is waking in the morning and thanking God, if there is such a thing, for the goodness of the Montavaldos—even if they were Mafiosi or money launderers or bankers responsible for the housing market crisis and the subsequent collapse of the world economy. After all, we all make mistakes. And even if they had hidden their money in foreign bank accounts and skedaddled just short of the feds' investigation, I understood and I forgave them. Because of the Montavaldos, I had a warm bed and room to hide in while I nursed my broken heart.

How did this happen? How did I get to this place, I wondered as I staggered out of another child-size bed in the minuscule guest room of this palatial penthouse. Blink, I was fourteen; blink, I'm here now. Was I stupid and pathetic, or crazy? Why had I believed in Donny, despite all his deceptions? He had stolen money he didn't even need from Mr. Smithson! Why on earth would I have believed that he would not steal my talent and hard work? Down, down I spiraled into a deep, black hole. If I didn't stop, there would be no coming up.

I opened my Redweld with my important papers and the packet of mail forwarded by the Moose Country Post Office. A good distraction. I would look things over with coffee.

The Montavaldos' kitchen was spotless and drenched in sun from a wall of windows looking out on a roof garden. I had to remind myself that I'd been invited as I searched through the custom-built mahogany cupboards for a mug and breakfast fixings.

Crows cawed as I boiled water, and I opened the roof garden door to see at least half a dozen of them perched on the railing around the penthouse, staring at me. "Hello, Zelda," they seemed to be saying. "We've been waiting for you." Then in one motion, they dove from the railing, down and down and out of sight.

It was a beautiful roof garden with big shady trees and planters full of flowers even this late in the season. If I had to be homeless, jobless, and broken-hearted, I couldn't do better than this for a hiding place. I buttered toast, scrambled eggs, and placed breakfast and my Redweld on a huge mahogany tray and took it outside.

Once settled at the picnic table under the shady tree, I inhaled warm food smells as I pulled a handful of papers and the packet of mail out of the Redweld. There was my list of rejected submissions, miscellaneous ideas for new articles, and Peggy's ancient "How It Is" list—cute. The mail was mostly junk, the telephone and electricity bills, and one from Principal Appleton. What could he want? I could not bear the thought of returning to Moose Country as a teaching assistant, but if he was begging me to come back, perhaps I should give it serious consideration. After all, it had been awfully nice of him not to have me arrested after the Walt Edelman incident. Maybe he had further forgiven me and was offering me my old teaching job.

I finished my toast, chewing each bite to a pulp, and I took a deep drink of coffee. Then I played with his letter, dreading opening it to have my fantasies punctured. But I also craved a quick solution to my present problem of unemployment, heartbreak, and homelessness. Perhaps I could simply go back to Moose Country, no questions asked.

That's when I remembered my stolen car. Reporting it did not seem wise since I had never registered the vehicle and my license was expired. I supposed I could get a bus, and maybe Principal Appleton would be so glad to have me back that he'd say, "Certainly, I'll be happy to pick you up. You can stay with me until you find a place to live. What time will you arrive?"

"Get real, Zelda," I may have said out loud. "No way is Appleton giving you your old job. And where will you live on a teaching assistant's salary?"

I finished my scrambled eggs and stared at Principal Appleton's letter. The humiliation of returning as a teaching assistant or the black hole of New York? Suddenly being a teaching assistant didn't seem so bad, and I ripped open the letter:

> *Dear Zelda,*
> *Can you please explain the enclosed?*
> *Yours truly,*
> *Albert Appleton*

Enclosed was a two-page bill.

In an attempt at redemption, I had left my stolen copy of the *Complete Works of Jack London* in the gate cabin. Had the Moose Country Library sent me a twenty-seven-years-overdue fine?

The invoice, addressed to my attention, was for two hundred thirty-five dollars from a New York law office. I turned to the second page: "Royalty past-due for one Christmas play performance of 'Dusty Rose.'"

Apparently my letter of twenty-five years ago had found Mike the poet.

I ripped the invoice into tiny pieces and threw them down the Montavaldos' garbage disposal. The gall of that man! That arrogant, using sonofabitch who had never paid me and had left me with his hotel bill! That poseur who had actually convinced the world of his specialness. That egotistical, pathological, self-serving, manipulative bastard—

And suddenly I realized who I was really talking about. Donny Sherman knew about the importance of contracts. He'd had me sign and unsign a mountain of them back in high school. He knew the importance of legal rights. My lack of contract was not an oversight or a lapse in memory or a promise not yet kept. Well, he wasn't going to get away with it again. Not with Zelda McFigg. No way would he take credit—and payment—for my work. I am not a stupid woman. This time I'd made a record of my efforts. There was the signed *O²* proposal and all my yellow legal pad notes. Oh God, I'd left the pad in the trash basket in Donny's guest room. I'd left the only handwritten record of my auteurship in the home of the thief!

Calm down, Zelda. Remember Tony Robbins's Three Pillars of Progress:

> *I. Focus & Clarity—I needed my pad back.*
> *II. Tools to Get Results—My action must be to return to Donny's apartment.*
> *III. Unlock What's Stopping Me—Donny's presence?*

Not a problem. I'd had no bad words with Donny. He probably didn't even know I was angry. I could simply call—No, no, a phone call would make him suspicious. I would just go back to the apartment this afternoon when I knew Donny would be out. He disappeared every day between two and dusk. When I'd asked where he went, he'd said, "Oh, you know, this and that, that and this"— translation: sex bars and porno movies; I believe the term is satyriasis. I was sure that the package he'd received was full of sex toys, and almost all of his laptop "favorites" were naked women sites.

So this was perfect. While Donny was out fornicating, I would visit. I would tell George the doorman that I'd forgotten something, and he would let me in. Piece of cake. Then I would retrieve the incontrovertible, legally viable evidence that *I*, not Mr. Donny Turn Bull Sherman, had created O^2, and Donny would never even know about it. I could play hardball, too, if need be. In fact, if it became necessary, I'd bypass Donny and present my notes straight to Miss Olga herself, unleashing my unlimited inner power and ensuring credit and at least enough compensation to live comfortably until I was eligible for Social Security.

Hurriedly I cleaned up the breakfast dishes, threw out that ridiculous "How It Is" list from Peggy as well as the rest of the mail, then I hightailed it downstairs.

"Taxi!" I snapped at the doorman in the lobby of the Montavaldos' building.

"Four-thirty-five East Sixty-fifth Street!" I commanded the driver. "And step on it."

"Hello!" I said to George the doorman, as he approached my cab. Upon recognizing me, his smile turned to disgust. I could remedy that. "I'm deeply sorry I didn't tip you, George," said I, reaching for my purse, and that's when I discovered I had forgotten it. "Well, another time then," I said, lumbering out of the taxi.

"Hey!" yelled the driver. "The fare! The fare!"

"George," said I in my most amiable former teacher's voice, "It seems I have forgotten my purse. Would you be so kind as to—"

But George stood solid, arms akimbo, in front of the taxi door as the driver, a large Sikh man, burst out of his door with such violence that he almost lost his turban. "Hey!" he yelled, colliding with George in an attempt to block me.

But I was a woman of unlimited power. I used the confusion as well as all two hundred thirty-seven of my pounds to barrel past the men. A linebacker could not have done it better. I ran into the building, into the open elevator, and before George or the driver could disentangle themselves from each other, I was on my way up to the sixteenth floor.

So what if George wouldn't let me in? Locked doors had never stopped Zelda McFigg. I would find a way in and I would retrieve my work product. And if necessary, I would go to court against the whole Olga Corporation. Templeton knew the truth. A "rewriter," Donny had called him; why he'd probably picked up where I'd left off; how else would Donny have graduated Yale? And Peggy had seen my contribution. She would represent me, Templeton would be my witness, and never again would Zelda McFigg be the uncredited, uncompensated ghost for an ungrateful recreant!

As the doors opened on the sixteenth floor, there was a deafening sound. A siren? An alarm system? "Mrs. Lambert!" I screamed. "For goodness sake, will you turn that off!" And as I ran toward apartment 16D, the second elevator opened and I was tackled by two security officers.

Chapter 37

Because I had no identification, the cops jailed me. After several hours in a cage with prostitutes and heroin addicts who were not nearly so well dressed as Matilda, I gave them Donny's phone number. But I could barely look at him when he arrived with my bail.

"Hi, Zelda," said he.

"Where's my contract?" said I.

Surprise only lasted a second, quickly replaced by a secret look of amused understanding, his black eyes sparkling like the mica boulders on the dirt road to his house. "You have got to be joking," he said. Then he laughed.

"I detest you," I hissed.

"She's crazy," he confided to the officers, smiling in that confused, self-deprecating way that convinced people that he wasn't a psychopath.

When Peggy arrived—because apparently I needed a lawyer—Donny smiled that way again. "She always had the hots for me," he told her. "I guess when I said no, it pushed her over the edge."

Lurleen Lagerfelt's crazed expression the day she got dragged to the loony bin filled my mind's eye, but, choosing my thoughts, controlling my responses, I said nothing. When Peggy looked at me, the pitying expression filled her whole face, but I didn't tell her that Donny had robbed her father and slept with her mother. All I said was, "Thanks for coming, Peggy. I will appreciate anything you can do."

"Scuse me, is one of you an attorney?" said an officer, entering with a clipboard and aerosol freshener which he sprayed in my direction.

"She is," said Donny, smiling dopily at Peggy.

"Can you both come with me?" said the cop. And everybody but the jail matron disappeared into another room.

To make a very long story a little less long, it seems they not only had discovered my arrest for the animal laboratory break-in and several minor shop-lifting incidents as well as a complaint about a missing case of Redweld expanding file envelopes and sundry office supplies, but there was a pleading by some man I'd never heard of named Seymour Slavin about the destruction of theater props in an obscure summer stock playhouse, a warrant for my arrest from Matilda the drug addict's ex-boyfriend for nonpayment of fees for his deplorable acting lessons, as well as an ancient missing persons report from a woman who claimed to be my mother. In all honesty, I do not know who she was. She was a frail, decrepit thing who cried a lot and said she was sorry. But she bore no resemblance to anyone I had ever met.

I spent one week in the psychiatric ward of Beth Israel Hospital on Sixteenth Street west of First Avenue—a charming place, about one step up from the animal lab, where fluorescent lights glared

24/7, no reading matter was allowed because it might be used as a weapon, but there was a blaring TV that ran nonstop in the visitors room. I shared this abode with a delightful group of lithium-chugging, saliva-drooling, zombie-walking incarcerates, one of whom yelled, "Let me out!" day and night, in a voice reminiscent of Mrs. Mendelson's jailed bird, Barnard.

During my stay, I seem to recall several visits from Peggy and one very strange one from Templeton where he peppered me with bizarre questions about the latest big-city transplants to Moose Country.

"Who cares about Moose Country?" I bellowed. "You're a talented boy. You should let it go, stop believing you're too small. For goodness sake, *do* something with your life!"

I do not know if Mr. Turn Bull Sherman ever tried to see me, because I had left a standing order with the desk matron that I did not wish to see him.

"He is a thief, you know," I confided in her. "He took credit for all of my writing. It was I, not he, who authored the *Moose Country Mutterer*. And did you know I have also just created a new magazine for the Olga Company?" But the matron, too, had been brainwashed. In order to convince her, I quoted story lists from my photographic memory of my yellow legal pad, but she merely smiled, certain that I was like the other inmates—crazy.

I tried to tell Peggy about all those years on the school paper, but all she said was "Yes, Zelda, I understand." I tried to tell her her father would always love her—even if she *did* give up horseback riding and she had always been so much more than a Vermont fashionista and I was sure Donny had loved her for all that. But she just gave me a funny look and asked how I'd feel about moving to a facility in Moose Country.

"You mean where they locked up Lagerfelt?" I said with amusement.

Peggy nodded.

It seems my soon-to-be-discontinued health insurance only covered me in Vermont, and New York was anxious to get rid of me so they wouldn't have to foot the bills.

Chapter 38

There were several benefits to the Vermont Facility, not the least of which was some surprising company.

"You are very fat," said Don Pedro, sitting down beside me for my first cardboard toast and rubber egg breakfast.

I see Brenda too. When she visits Don Pedro, she always sneaks me several packages of peanut butter and cheese cracker sandwiches which I share with a somewhat bald woman they call "the cat lady" because when they found her, she was alone with no food on what she called an organic farm, knee-deep in feral cats.

"Matilda?" I said, thinking I recognized her baby-doll face through the weathered creases and dead eyes.

"You must have me mistaken for someone else," she said, pulling out a wisp of ravaged grey hair (I believe the term is trichotillomania.) "Would you be a dear and invest in my organic commune? Thank you for the crackers. They left me with no food, you know. I must get home to feed the cats. Ta-ta."

Also, there's Lurleen Lagerfelt. They call her a therapist, but we both know she visits for the tune-ups. We've become quite chummy actually. She finally gave me the inside poop on her promiscuity back in the day. Something about her fear of being alone—about feeling so afraid of how afraid she was that she thought if she felt even one drop of it, she'd go mad, so instead she had sex. It was a long, complicated, sordid story and her eyes looked so needy and pleading—especially during the part about how, when she finally felt the fear, how even though her periods stopped and her beautiful hair fell out, it was all worth it because somehow that was what got her out of her black, lonely hole and back to sanity—so to be a friend, I reciprocated with an amusing account of my many years of syncopated investigative excursions. I knew it was tempting fate and may have even extended my stay here—approaching my second year, as of this writing—after I overheard Lagerfelt whispering to Powers that Be, "She's not ready"—but it is cruel to let a person who has shared her deepest shame and vulnerability think that her audience is silently superior. Also I simply had to vent.

As in the loony bin on Sixteenth Street, we are denied books, magazines, or any object that could be slung, thrown, or used as a deadly weapon to bash someone's head in. So it was on the incessantly blaring television in the rec room that I got the news—fittingly on the *Miss Olga Show*.

It seems that Templeton recently authored a groundbreaking, bestselling work of creative nonfiction called *The Secret Lives of Rural Americans*, illuminating the neuroses and foibles of the burgeoning yuppie colonizers who have gentrified small towns in the Northeastern US of A.

Apparently my articles that had been so rudely rejected by *Ubiquity* had not only reached Templeton, but had been read and photocopied by him. And to add insult to plagiarism, that rewriting rat boy had created a character called Zena—an overweight, would-be tap dancer who reads children's literature and secretly keeps diaries about everybody in her small town, the exploits of which form the body of the book.

"Is Zena based on a real person?" asked Olga, her eyes glittering with interest as she held up the latest O^2—where the chapter on rural kids was excerpted.

"Oh God, no," laughed Templeton in his best imitation of Donny Sherman being self-deprecating. "No, Olga, I'm afraid that's just the product of my extremely vivid writer's imagination. Zena is just a symbol of that frustrated little kid in all of us. You know, I believe, if we're honest about those dark, secret places we have inside—those places we hope nobody else sees—we all believe that we're just not good enough or we don't fit in. Zena personifies the 'every-loser,' if you will. She's in all of us. It's the human condition."

"Do you really believe that?" said Olga, incredulous. "Do most people believe they are losers?"

"Everybody but me," quipped Templeton. "But seriously. Why else would people spend so much energy pretending and comparing themselves to others? Why else would winning be so important and failure so devastating?"

Olga thought about this and then abruptly changed the subject. "Do you know what my favorite part of the book is?"

"Tell me," said Templeton, relaxing back in his chair like Donny the day we went to see *HAIR*.

Olga gleefully flipped through the excerpted article in O^2, making sure to flash the cover to the cameras, and then she read:

> *Perhaps the only person who was not affected by the pressure and pretense of having the American dream was the town drunk. He lived alone in the woods with his grandson and died, with virtually no possessions, on the roof of his outhouse where he liked to sleep. "Why did he sleep on the roof?" Zena*

asked the grandson. The grandson thought hard. Then finally he answered, "It was something about the stars."

"Sky burial," Templeton said contemplatively. "It's the Tibetan way."

"I just love that," said Olga, closing the magazine with a sigh and grinning at Templeton. "It's as if the stars gave him hope for something better, something greater, some purpose to it all."

You may recall that I have a mouse phobia. Odd as it may seem, I have no such fear of rats. I would like to kill the rat boy. I would like to put him in a cage on top of an outhouse with nothing but a cheap plastic plate of arsenic-laced chocolate chip cookies and no milk. Then I would pull up a lawn chair and watch. I would watch as he died slowly, feeling the pain, feeling the effect of his crimes, incontrovertibly aware of his impending death and who had caused it. And when it was finally done—sky burial, my ass!—I would incinerate his malignant carcass and toss it into a mud bog where I'd run it over several times with an old VW bug.

But only a crazy person would do that.

So instead I have chosen to set the record straight. I am writing this memoir—during supervised sessions in the Vermont Facility computer room—under my own name, Zelda McFigg, in order to let it be incontrovertibly known that this is *my* life. I am a real person, not a symbol or a personification or a figment of a rat boy's vivid imagination.

I would further like to say that, even though I chose to throw out the grand "How It Is" list and lean a tad north of the plumb line, I now see that I am no loser—any more than you are. In my opinion, winning and hope are highly over-rated. Now that I have failed, there is nothing to lose. So even though I have gone down several dress sizes from a diet of institutional cardboard crap, I am neither elated nor feeling pressure to be thin. Nor do I wish to celebrate my habit of slowly eating myself to death; I will enter no Miss Plus-Size America Contests, but will instead gradually, without fanfare, evaporate my excess.

"But why, Zelda?" you may be saying. "Why have you waited so long, gone so far, made so many mistakes?"

To which I answer, I really couldn't tell you. Nor do I really care. I do not worry about my purpose or the meaning of it all or why things happen. Those things are none of my business, and I've lost my taste for snooping. Who cares if Don Pedro has more money than I, or if Lagerfelt is thinner and has more sex? I do not worry about my position in the world or winning, because what is there to win? It is a relief to fail and be satisfied with what is. It is a relief to wake up from the American dream.

Speaking of which, I know that many of you—particularly you American dreamers—are judging me harshly, but please hear me out. Yes, I have done some despicable things, but I am not a despicable person. I am merely a person who once tried to be a friend to a boy who was in trouble. A boy I sometimes miss. A boy who couldn't love anyone best.

"What could *you* know?" you scoff. "What on earth could a forty-nine and one-quarter-year-old overweight virgin know about love?"

Here's what I know: This book a testament of conviction and truth—my conviction, my truth—which says that no matter what

New Age gurus tell you, love does not cancel hate. Or hurt. Or resentment. Or a desire for rectification. I am living proof of that. That boy that I sometimes miss, he also disgusts me. And even though I want no contact, I cherish the fact that we are forever connected. Yes, I want him to hurt, but I also long for him to succeed, to be happy, to know love. I have always wanted these things—from the day I met him to now.

So you see I *do* know something: I know that even though I may have done it badly, even if it made me somewhat crazy, even if it was unreciprocated, mocked, and pitied, I am grateful that I took the risk.

"You must be nuts," say you.

"So be it, so be it," say I.

"By why, why?" you implore.

"So simple," I reply. "Because no matter how much it costs or hurts, I am glad that I have loved."